"Come home with me, now. I want to make love to you, Fiona."

Make love to you. As though the shaft of an arrow had pierced her heart, Karyn went utterly still in the man's arms. Although, she thought distantly, nothing could have stopped the air heaving in her lungs, the pulse throbbing in her ears. Or the pangs of desire, unrelieved, that ached in her belly.

In a kiss that seemed to have gone on forever, she'd traveled to a place she'd never been before. She, Karyn Marshall.

Not Fiona Talbot.

"I know you want me," the man whispered, running his finger down her cheek and tracing the soft curve of her lips until she gave another of those unquenchable shudders of response. "You want me as much as I want you."

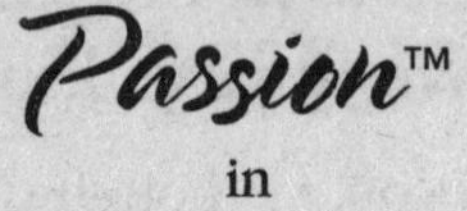

in

Harlequin Presents®

Looking for sophisticated stories that **sizzle**?
Wanting a read that has a little extra **spice**?

Pick up a Presents Passion™ novel—
where **seduction** is *guaranteed!*

Available only from Harlequin Presents®

Coming in July:
Savage Awakening
by Anne Mather
#2477

Sandra Field

THE ENGLISH ARISTOCRAT'S BRIDE

Passion™

TORONTO • NEW YORK • LONDON
AMSTERDAM • PARIS • SYDNEY • HAMBURG
STOCKHOLM • ATHENS • TOKYO • MILAN • MADRID
PRAGUE • WARSAW • BUDAPEST • AUCKLAND

ISBN 0-373-12465-1

THE ENGLISH ARISTOCRAT'S BRIDE

First North American Publication 2005.

This edition published by arrangement with Harlequin Books S.A.

www.eHarlequin.com

Printed in U.S.A.

CHAPTER ONE

HER sister lived in this house. The sister she had never met, whose existence she'd discovered a scant four weeks ago.

Karyn Marshall stepped deeper into the shadows of the trees. Should anyone glance out of one of the tall windows set in mellow, rose-pink brick, she was safely hidden from view. Skulking like a common thief, she thought with a shiver. Watching and waiting.

It wasn't just a house. It was a mansion. Wisteria drooped its delicate blooms all the way up to the second story; there were stables to one side and a four-car garage with a cobbled driveway. Every detail was perfect, yet served only to increase her unease.

She was afraid. Far too afraid to announce her presence.

Her twin sister and only sibling, Fiona Talbot, lived in this house, whose name was Willowbend. For Fiona, Willowbend was home, along with a luxury beyond Karyn's imagining. Karyn glanced down at her plain linen slacks and tailored shirt, clothes she'd thought would be entirely adequate for this meeting. An evening dress would have been more appropriate; not that she owned one.

She'd given away all her dresses after Steve had died.

Karyn shrank back against the tree trunk as a woman in a glowing red gown suddenly appeared in one of the windows. An older woman; even at this distance, Karyn could discern the twinkle of diamonds encircling her throat. Was this Clarissa Talbot, Fiona's adoptive mother? The woman turned her head to speak to someone in the room, then disappeared. A moment later, a uniformed butler drew long curtains across the window.

A butler. Karyn bit back a quiver of hysterical laughter. This was an English country mansion. Of course they'd have a butler.

Why, oh, why, hadn't she written first, to tell the family of her existence? That way, she'd have been an expected guest who could have walked confidently up the driveway and knocked on the front door.

She hadn't written because she'd worried that the Talbots would tell her to stay away. To leave the past where it belonged, buried and forgotten.

If only she wasn't so desperate to meet her unknown twin, to assuage some of the terrible loneliness of the last few months…

Behind Karyn, something rustled in the undergrowth. She whirled, her heart leaping like a startled rabbit's, every nerve on edge. A twig snapped. She strained her eyes, trying to penetrate the dense tangle of shrubs and trees, and to her dismay saw a darker shadow climbing the little slope that led up to the garden. Coming her way.

A man. Whistling softly under his breath, finding his way through the gloomy woods with the ease of familiarity.

Her eyes flicked around her. She could have tried to hide, ducking behind the nearest oak tree and hoping for the best. But her raincoat was light beige, as were her trousers, and the odds of remaining unseen far too small. So she stood her ground, lifting her chin. She might look like a thief. But there was no need to behave like one.

The man was only a few feet away from her. He was tall, with hair black as night; dressed casually in jeans and a sweater, he moved with a feline grace that added one more layer to her fear. She'd read about poachers who prowled the woods after dark. Was he one of them? A lawbreaker? She should have hidden. Or run. While she had the chance.

Then, suddenly, the man saw her. He stopped dead in his tracks, his eyes, dark as his hair, trained on her face. ''Fiona,'' he said softly, ''what are you doing out here?''

Karyn's breath had lodged in her throat; she couldn't have said a word to save her soul. At the inn where she was staying in the village of Droverton, the landlord on his first sight of her had called her ''Miss Fiona,'' and his initial disbelief had been all too obvious when she'd said she was Karyn Marshall, a tourist from eastern Canada. He'd looked, she remembered quite clearly, downright suspicious; and hadn't behaved with any of the friendliness she'd expected to find in a little village inn.

Now the man who'd appeared out of the woods was confirming what the landlord's behavior had suggested: she and Fiona must be identical twins. Must look so very much alike that one of them could be mistaken for the other.

The man had stepped a little closer. He was well over six feet tall, broad-shouldered and long-legged, making Karyn feel both feminine and fragile in a way she didn't care for. Although his face was shadowed, she could see that it was strongly hewn, handsome and full of character. Character? Much too wishywashy a word, she thought breathlessly. How about ruthlessness? Power? Charisma? Cemented together with a compellingly male dose of sexiness. It took all her pride not to step back, and all her willpower to keep her eyes from fastening on the carved sensuality of his mouth.

Think, Karyn. Think.

Her throat might have closed as though a hand was clamped tight around it. But she didn't have to shut her brain off as well. The man had called her Fiona, not Miss

Fiona. So he knew her sister well. Perhaps, just perhaps, he'd be her way into Willowbend.

She might succeed, after all, in meeting her twin this very evening; and if she had to use this black-haired man to do so, she would.

Rafe Holden had been thinking about Fiona as he wended his way through the trees. He'd hoped to make it to Willowbend in time for dinner that evening; but his flight from Athens had been delayed, and he'd phoned Clarissa to tell her not to expect him.

Then, breaking into his thoughts as he climbed the slope, something had alerted him to another presence in the woods. When he glanced up, he saw Fiona immediately; she was standing against the oak tree that the pair of them had often climbed as children. He, seven years older and always the leader; and always protective of his little blond, blue-eyed neighbor.

"Fiona," he said, "what are you doing out here?"

As he waited for her to answer, his feet sank gently into the rich humus of last autumn's leaves, new ferns brushing his knees. His gaze sharpened and he stepped a little closer. She looked frightened. More than frightened, as though something had knocked her right off balance, striking her dumb. If Clarissa had been at her again, there'd be hell to pay. He'd see to that.

He closed the distance between them in three swift strides and took her in his arms. Her body was taut. Her scent was new, more complex and more sensuous than he was used to. He liked it. Liked it very much. Her hair was different, too. Astonishingly different. For as long as he could remember, Fiona had obeyed her mother's strictures to let her hair grow all the way down her back; she often wore it pulled away from her face in a long braid. Virginal, he'd occasionally thought. Untouched. Just as Clarissa wanted Fiona to be.

But now her hair was cut short, feathered to her face in soft curls that made her look like another woman. A more sophisticated woman; and again that word sensuous came to Rafe's mind. Her decision to lop off her braid intrigued him, and he was certainly into encouraging any rebellions on her part. He said, bending his head to kiss her cheek, "I like the haircut—what made you do it? I bet that got your mother's goat."

He liked holding Fiona. It was like coming home to all that was familiar, to the friendship they'd shared for years, their bonds of a shared history and a deep love of the landscape where they'd both grown up. He rubbed his cheek gently against the softness of her hair, wanting only to soothe her. Clarissa Talbot on the warpath was a force to be reckoned with.

Then, to his astonishment, her head shifted and almost inadvertently his mouth found hers. Her lips were cool, their touch tentative; her slender frame, in a raincoat he'd never seen before, felt as rigid as the ghastly Greek nymphs Douglas Talbot had stationed throughout the azalea garden. Against her mouth, he whispered, "It's okay…you can relax now. I'm here, and I'm on your side."

One of his hands was cupping her nape. Wisps of blond hair, soft and silky, teased his fingers. She made a tiny sound in her throat, and almost insensibly her mouth softened under his. There were layers upon layers to her scent, each of them encouraging him to explore further.

Which was something he'd never thought of doing before. Certainly never felt driven to do. For wasn't Fiona his oldest friend? Only once in his life had he known the fire and recklessness of a passion that had swept him off his feet, and the results had devastated him in a way he'd never forgotten, and had no wish to repeat. For him, Fiona's strongest attraction was how she represented all the comforts of familiarity: the ease, the lack of demand and the total trust.

He could live without passion. Once burned, twice shy. Or, more accurately in his case, once burned, permanently shy.

By now her body had softened, too, her shoulder under his palm fractionally less tight. Still with infinite care, Rafe drew her closer, sliding his hand under her coat to find her shoulder and knead it gently through the folds of her shirt. She even felt different, he thought in an unquenchable shaft of excitement. All of a sudden he didn't want the feel of fabric; he wanted her skin to his. Heat to heat.

His kiss deepened, the pressure of his mouth seeking more from her. In a sunburst of shocked delight he realized she was giving him exactly what he was asking, opening to him, yielding. Her hands were pressed to his chest, their warmth penetrating his pores. Slowly, as though she were savoring every moment, her palms slid upward to encircle the back of his neck, where her fingers buried themselves in his hair. He was the one who should have got a haircut, Rafe thought dimly. He'd planned to, but the meetings at his new hotel had taken longer than he'd expected.

Then he stopped thinking altogether as he felt the first, swift dart of her tongue to his. Instantly he met her, feeding on the wet, slick heat of her mouth, enticed by its sweetness. He wrapped his arms around her, pulling her toward him, her pliancy like a flame in his arms, her startled gasp of pleasure potent as the roar of a waterfall on the fells. How could he possibly have guessed that so much ardor was hidden under her delicacy, beneath that air she wore of remoteness and untouchability?

She'd never shown it to him before.

His groin had hardened with fierce intent; he shifted away from her, afraid she would withdraw from fear or shyness. However, in a fierce mingling of gratitude and sheer lust, he felt her press her hips into his, as though she, too, craved to do away with the barriers of clothing and civilized restraint. Yearned to belong to him in the most primitive of ways.

Desperate to touch her, Rafe tugged her shirt from her waistband and thrust his hand under it. Her skin was like the finest silk, her ribs impossibly fragile. When he found the swell of her breast, firm and warm under the sheerest of lace, its tip was hard as a small stone. She moaned again as he teased her nipple; all the while his tongue played with hers, their lips locked together in a searing commitment to give each other pleasure.

From a long way away, he was aware of her tearing at his shirt; then felt the dizzying heat of her fingers flat against his chest, tangled in his body hair. His heart was pounding like a farrier's hammer; his own nipples hardened to her touch. He nibbled at her lower lip, his teeth scraping her tongue, his emotions churning as she trembled in his embrace in mute and total surrender. Could he die of such ecstasy?

He wanted her here. Now. On the ground, against the tree, he didn't care. Had he ever felt such explosive desire, such hot, fierce hunger?

But he couldn't take her here. Not Fiona. Not in sight of Willowbend. His breath sobbing in his chest, Rafe said urgently, "Come home with me now, to Stoneriggs. I want to make love to you, Fiona." His voice warmed with laughter. "In a bed. Not on the ground under the oak trees—you deserve better than that."

Make love to you. As though the shaft of an arrow had pierced her to the heart, Karyn went utterly still in the man's arms. Although, she thought distantly, nothing could have stopped the air heaving in her lungs, the pulse throbbing in her ears. Or the pangs of desire, unrelieved, that ached in her belly.

In a kiss that seemed to have gone on forever, she'd traveled to a place she'd never been before. She, Karyn Marshall.

Not Fiona Talbot.

"I know you want me," the man whispered, running his fingers down her cheek and tracing the soft curve of her lips until she gave another of those unquenchable shudders of response. "You want me as much as I want you."

Distraught, horrified, Karyn struggled to get her breath under control, to find her voice amid the turmoil in her body. What had happened to her? How could she have let a simple kiss go this far without blurting out who she was?

But before she could even find the words, let alone speak them, a chorus of excited barking split the silence of the woods. From the undergrowth a pack of dogs burst into the open and hurled themselves joyously on the man who was still clasping her in his arms. Their weight threw him sideways. Seeing her chance, Karyn yanked herself free. Obeying instinct, she whirled and raced for the woods.

"Get down, Sandy! Randall, down! For God's sake, when are my parents ever going to teach you any manners? Charlotte, off!"

If Karyn had learned one thing during that devastating kiss, it was that this man took what he wanted: he wouldn't be delayed for long. She ran for her life, tumbling down the slope and leaping over a stream that roiled between rocks slippery with moss. The woods were thicker now, and the sun had set. Seeking the shadows, jumping over fallen trunks, she ran on, deeper and deeper into the trees.

She was headed in the general direction of the village, that much she knew, and for which she was pitifully grateful.

"Fiona! Fiona, come back."

His voice was fainter, masked by the leaves, the rattle of the stream and the barking dogs. Desperately Karyn increased her pace, until her ribs hurt and her chest was starved for air. Branches lashed her coat, her hands warding them from her face. Would the dogs follow her? Lead him to her?

Then what?

It was her nightmare all over again, she thought with sudden, sickening clarity: the nightmare that had recurred with ominous regularity ever since her husband Steve's death. In it she was running for her life through the darkness...

All too abruptly, the woods thinned and with a whimper of fear she burst into an open field. A stone wall loomed ahead of her, curving around to the left; sheep were huddled like small boulders on the other side.

The road to the village, she remembered, ran alongside this field. If she could cross the road, she could follow the woods on the far side until she came to the cluster of houses. Once she was at the inn, she'd be safe.

Safe from what? A nightmare? Or from the man in the woods?

He hadn't exactly attacked her. She'd been the one who'd gone on the attack. Who'd laced her tongue with his in open invitation and pushed her hips against his.

With a moan of despair Karyn scrambled toward the nearest wall which, she now saw, edged the woods all the way back toward Willowbend. A metal gate was inset where the wall met the field. The harsh whine of hinges scraping her nerves, she unlatched the gate, swung it open and eased through, carefully shutting it behind her. The sheep paid her no attention whatsoever.

The road was empty, its grassy verges fragrant with wildflowers. Her lungs still fighting for air, she crossed it as quickly as she could, easing into the shrubbery on the other side and scurrying toward the lights of the village. The man who'd kissed her had come through the woods; at least he didn't have a car in which to pursue her.

She'd kissed him with a seductive intimacy that Steve, even in the early days of courtship, had never elicited from her. Yet she didn't even know the man's name.

What difference? She didn't need to know his name. She just had to make sure she never saw him again.

She'd reached the first house, stone like so many of the houses here, its tiny front garden jammed with a riot of delphiniums, foxgloves, daisies and poppies. After drawing her coat tighter around her, Karyn pulled her headscarf from her pocket to cover her hair and as much of her face as she could.

The sidewalk, to her great relief, was empty: to have been mistaken for Fiona for the third time that day would have been more than she could bear. To her greater relief, the dour landlord of the inn was nowhere in sight when she pushed open the door; the wood-paneled counter with its tarnished collection of horse brasses was deserted, although she could hear the echo of laughter from the pub. She sneaked up the stairs, unlocked her door and slipped into her room. Quickly she snubbed the latch. Then she leaned back on the panels, letting out her breath in a shuddering sigh.

Her knees were trembling from her flight. Her trousers were flecked with bracken and dirt. She felt both exhausted and horribly wired. But she was alone. And she was safe.

She'd learned two things this evening. That Fiona lived

a privileged life amid surroundings of exquisite beauty; and that her sister had a lover, a black-haired man who had—under the assumption that Karyn was Fiona—kissed her as though there was no tomorrow.

No, Karyn thought sickly, levering herself away from the door and dragging off her coat. She'd learned three things. She'd learned that passion, which she'd thought had died within her long before she was widowed, wasn't dead after all. It had taken just one kiss from a total stranger to show that her sexuality, far from being dead, had merely been slumbering. Waiting to be reawoken.

Never again, she thought. Never again. Sinking down on the old brass bed, Karyn buried her face in her hands.

It took Rafe nearly five minutes to get the six dogs sitting in a circle at his feet, gazing up at him adoringly, their pink tongues flopping from sharp-toothed jaws. "You're idiots," he said coldly. "I love my mother dearly, but on the subject of dogs we differ. I'd have paid ten times over for obedience classes, and will she do it? *Oh darling, they listen to me, and that's what counts.*"

Right. They listened to his mother when she had a pocketful of dog biscuits, that's when they listened. In a resigned voice Rafe went on, "Okay, we're going to Fiona's. I'm locking you in the garage and I'm expecting you to keep your big mouths shut. Have you got that?"

Charlotte flopped down on her belly and rolled over. With an exasperated sigh Rafe headed for the house. In a way, he was almost glad of the six dogs now trooping at his heels as though they'd never leaped up on him and stopped a kiss that had overturned his world. What would have happened next? Would Fiona have gone with him to Stoneriggs and made love with him in his big bed?

Maybe not, he thought with a touch of grimness. After

all, hadn't she pulled free and run for the woods as though all the hounds of hell were after her? Had she so quickly regretted that surge of passion, wishing it had never happened?

He could have gone after her. But the dogs would have liked nothing better than another mad dash through the trees, and the odds of finding her were slim. Besides, he couldn't bear the thought of chasing her down like a fugitive.

His whole body was one big ache of frustration. His jaw set, Rafe marched past the perennial garden and across the forecourt of topiaried yews and formal clipped boxwood. He loathed topiary. Clarissa's gardener was never going to get within a mile of Stoneriggs.

He ushered the dogs into the garage and shut the door firmly, ignoring their downcast faces. He'd walk them home once he'd seen Clarissa and done his level best to find out what had upset Fiona. The haircut. He'd be willing to bet it was the haircut.

What had brought about that particular rebellion?

After cursorily rapping the large brass knocker against the door, Rafe let himself in. His boots were muddy from the stream, and his jeans wouldn't meet with Clarissa's approval; but he'd needed the exercise of walking over here from Stoneriggs after the day he'd had. He shucked off his boots, and heard Clarissa call from the dining room, ''Is that you, Rafe?''

''Sorry I'm so late,'' he called back, and walked into the vast living room with its array of Victorian ceramics, several of which he'd been tempted to knock—accidentally, of course—off their pedestals. There was only one person in the room. She was standing by the fireplace with a Spode cup in her hand; emerald earrings shot green fire as she turned her head.

Fiona.

Her long hair was drawn into an elegant twist on the back of her head. Her dress was a slim pencil of leaf-green.

Rafe's breath hissed through his teeth. Was he losing his mind?

Not stopping to think, he strode across the room. Taking the cup from her hand, he plunked it down on the priceless Chippendale table, took her in his arms and kissed her hard on the mouth.

No flame of response. No flick of her tongue. No matching heat, body to body.

No surrender.

Only her jerk of shock and sudden withdrawal, her hands warding him off. The sweet naiveté of lilies of the valley drifted to his nostrils, rather than subtle layers of scent that teased all his senses. As he wrenched his mouth free, Fiona gasped, "Rafe! Whatever's wrong with you?"

Before he could think of a word to say, she added in genuine horror, "What if Mother had seen us?"

"Even your mother must know that old friends kiss each other on occasion."

"That wasn't just a friendly kiss!"

"Maybe it's time for a change."

"But you've never kissed me like that. Ever."

He had. Only minutes before, under the shadow of the oak tree. Hadn't he?

His head whirling, Rafe said, "I need a drink."

"The coffee's freshly brewed." Her cheeks bright pink, Fiona indicated the ornate sterling pot on a tray by the hearth.

"Whiskey," he said tersely, and poured himself a triple from the crystal decanter on the sideboard.

"What's the matter?" Fiona said, distressed. "I don't

understand why you're behaving like this. Didn't Athens go well?''

He swallowed a hefty gulp of Glenfiddich, gazing at her broodingly. Fiona, well-known friend of so many years. Slim, beautiful, exquisitely groomed, her blue eyes like the delphiniums in the garden, her brows arched like the wings of birds. And her hair, in its thick coil on the back of her head, its wheaten gleam under the chandelier.

It wasn't Fiona he'd kissed under the trees. Obviously.

So who had he kissed? And where had she gone, that woman who'd looked enough like Fiona to be her sister, yet who'd responded to him as though she was his soul mate? Meant for him, and for him alone, calling to his blood as though he'd known her all his life.

He'd never seen her before this evening. He might never see her again.

''Darlings!'' Clarissa said, sweeping into the room in a rustle of taffeta.

''Hello, Clarissa,'' Rafe said, and dutifully kissed her expensively scented cheek.

''Lovely to see you, Rafe.'' She smiled charmingly at his jeans and socked feet. ''Even in deshabille. How was Athens?''

He'd recently opened a new resort several miles south of the city, one more addition to the international chain of luxury hotels that he owned and managed. ''Ironing out a few wrinkles,'' he said casually. ''Well worth the trip. You're looking lovely, Clarissa.''

From the doorway, Douglas Talbot said bluffly, ''I bought her that dress in London. It suits her rather well, don't you think?''

If Clarissa had the brittle beauty of a Dresden statuette, Douglas was a Toby jug. Rotund, outwardly hearty, Douglas was also, as Rafe knew all too well, a rabid social climber with a tendency to bully. Yet he adored his wife and would have done anything for her.

Rafe said smoothly, "A delightful dress, Clarissa, to which you more than do justice. Little wonder you have such a beautiful daughter."

Fiona's smile was almost natural; quite plainly, she'd decided Rafe's kiss was best ignored. Douglas poured himself a drink, asking a shrewd question about the political situation in Greece, and the evening proceeded along its predictable path. A couple of hours later Rafe took his leave, for once unamused when Fiona's parents tactfully left him alone with her. Clarissa and Douglas wanted much more than friendship between himself and their daughter; they wanted him to marry Fiona. Douglas, to put it bluntly, was applying the crudest of pressures toward that end.

He, Rafe, wasn't going to be pushed around by Douglas. Although, at the time, hadn't that kiss under the trees made the thought of marrying Fiona a lot more plausible?

Except for two small details. The woman hadn't been Fiona and the kiss had gotten way out of hand.

He was going around in circles, he thought furiously. Like a dog chasing its tail. Striving to sound casual, he said, "Am I taking you shopping tomorrow, Fiona?"

"In Coverdale, if you don't mind."

"No problem. I'll pick you up around ten?"

"That'd be lovely." With the shyness that normally Rafe found endearing, she reached up and brushed her lips to his cheek. "I'll see you tomorrow."

His pulses didn't even stir. Nothing. Absolutely nothing. Rafe patted her on the shoulder and let himself out. The dogs surged out of the shed, and he set off across the gardens behind the house. After closing the gate behind him, he took the path that meandered from Willowbend's more civilized surroundings to the open fells. The moon had risen over the trees, Venus a small steady light just below it.

Venus, goddess of love.

He loved Fiona, Rafe thought soberly. She was a dear friend he'd known all his life. But he wouldn't even have entertained the idea of marrying her if it hadn't in many ways suited him. He was thirty-three years old, ready to settle down and raise a family, and who better to do that with than Fiona? She'd never betray him as Celine had done all those years ago.

He'd bet every one of his hotels on that.

If he married Fiona, he'd also be rescuing Douglas from a series of disastrous investments. His eyes narrowed. A little financial leverage wasn't a bad thing to have should Douglas become his father-in-law. Rafe was several times smarter than Douglas and could be ten times as ruthless, and he'd have no hesitation in using any weapon at his command to free Fiona from her parents' smothering hold: a hold Fiona was too sweet and trusting to see, let alone counter.

He hadn't yet mentioned the word marriage to Fiona. He'd needed time to think about it first.

The path left the trees for the open fields. To the west Rafe could see the turrets and spires of Holden Castle, where he'd grown up. Eight years ago he'd had it extensively renovated as a five-star hotel and installed his parents as managers, to their enormous gratification. If Joan and Reginald Holden added a certain eccentricity to the castle, so be it. The customers didn't seem to mind.

He'd take the dogs back to his mother, then head home to Stoneriggs.

The moon had disappeared behind a cloud. But Rafe knew every footstep of the way, and walked confidently westward, Charlotte demurely trotting at his heels as though she'd never heard of misbehavior.

Why hadn't the woman, whoever she was, told him she wasn't Fiona? Why had she been hiding in the grounds of Willowbend in the first place? And why had she kissed him until he hadn't been able to think with anything except his hormones?

He swore under his breath. Rafe was no stranger to women throwing themselves at him; he was, after all, filthy rich and—so he'd been told—sexy to boot. But the woman couldn't possibly have known he'd be coming through the woods toward Willowbend. He hadn't even known it himself until after his flight delay.

He didn't like being made a fool of.

Didn't like the fact that passion could still take him unawares? Was that the crux of the matter?

He didn't want passion. Its betrayals were too cruel.

Tomorrow afternoon, after he'd taken Fiona home from the shopping expedition, he was going to get some answers to all his questions. In a village the size of Droverton, it shouldn't be difficult to find someone who so closely resembled Fiona. She had some explaining to do, that unknown woman. She owed him that much.

Maybe he would marry Fiona, he thought trenchantly, rounding a crag where a stream fell in a series of gurgling waterfalls. Assuming she'd have him. Marrying Fiona would ensure his personal life was entirely and happily predictable. Unlike the tempestuous ups and downs of his affair with Celine.

Unlike the tempestuous kiss in the woods?

There'd be no repeat of that, he thought grimly. He'd make it his business to forget the blond-haired witch who'd woven a spell around him under the shadow of the oak trees.

The sooner the better.

CHAPTER TWO

THAT night Karyn slept about as badly as it was possible for anyone to sleep. She did sleep. She knew that, because all too clearly she could remember fragments of dreams whose eroticism horrified her in the cool light of morning. But she also spent far too long wide-awake, her body on fire with needs she was determined to deny. Tossing and turning, she'd found every lump in the mattress and had heard every creak as the old building was buffeted by the night winds.

At some point in the middle of the night, as she stared wide-eyed at the low ceiling, Karyn had finally admitted to herself that being kissed, in all good faith, by the man who was Fiona's lover had further complicated her own compulsive need to meet her sister. Wasn't it all too likely that in meeting Fiona she'd meet him as well? How would she ever face him? Shake his hand and say *How do you do, so nice to see you again?* She groaned aloud, wishing with all her heart that she'd been rational and sensible and four weeks ago had written a letter to Fiona about her proposed visit.

She hadn't. So what was she going to do instead? Phone the Talbots this morning and ask for a meeting? Or write a letter and have it hand-delivered to Willowbend? She had to do one or the other. She couldn't just hang around the village on the off-chance that she'd bump into Fiona on the street; that wouldn't be fair to either of them. And she'd come too far at too great an expense to simply turn tail and flee.

What was she, a coward? No way. She was going to meet her sister, no matter what it took.

A bath in rather tepid water, choosing her most becoming summer dress and applying makeup all helped to restore Karyn's spirits. Okay, so last night had been a disastrous beginning to her quest. This was a new day, and she was going to begin afresh.

She snacked on an apple and some granola bars she'd stashed in her luggage, not wanting to face the landlord or any of the villagers now that she knew about the resemblance between herself and Fiona. In the little desk by the window she found a pad of yellowing notepaper and some envelopes. She sat down, took out her pen and, her tongue caught between her teeth, began to write.

It took several false starts before Karyn was satisfied with her letter. She folded it carefully and stuck it in one of the envelopes. Just as she got up from the desk, stretching the tension from her shoulders, someone rapped on the door.

She gave a nervous start, staring at the door in horror. The black-haired man from the woods was standing on the other side. She knew it. Who else could it be?

The landlord. Of course. Come on, Karyn, smarten up.

She marched over to the door and pulled it open. The man glaring at her in the hallway was almost a caricature: scarcely an inch taller than herself, round as a barrel, clad in a tweed suit with a tweed hat clasped in his pudgy hands. But, she realized rapidly, there was nothing remotely funny about the look in his eyes. Her smile dying on her lips, she said, "Yes? Can I help you?"

"My name is Douglas Talbot. You are, I presume, Miss Karyn Marshall?"

"Yes." He looked ready to give her a hard right to the

chin, and somehow this freed Karyn's tongue. "Although I'm not sure how you know my name."

"I wish to speak to you in private. May I come in?"

Her heart hammering in her rib cage, Karyn said calmly, "Of course, Mr. Talbot," and gestured him toward the chair by the desk. Quickly she picked up the letter and tossed it on the bed before closing the door. Then, there being no other option, she sat down on the bed and folded her cold hands in her lap.

The chair creaked ominously as Douglas Talbot sat down. He put his hat on the desk. "You can start by telling me exactly what you're doing here."

Karyn said pleasantly, "I'd be pleased to. But first I'd like to know how you got my name."

"The landlord phoned me last night to tell me you'd booked into the inn, and that you looked exactly like my daughter, Fiona. I want to know what game you're up to."

Karyn clamped firmly on her temper; losing it wouldn't advance her cause. "I'm sure you know why I'm here," she said. "I'm Fiona's twin sister. I—"

"Balderdash."

With a faint flicker of humor, Karyn realized she'd never actually heard anyone use that word before. She said flatly, "You asked why I was here. I'm trying to tell you. But if you won't listen, we're wasting each other's time."

Calculation flicked across Douglas's red face; clearly he hadn't expected any argument from her. "Then why don't you tell me your story? I'm sure you've had lots of time to concoct it."

"I'll tell you the truth," Karyn said.

As Douglas gave a rude snort, she tried to organize her thoughts. Douglas Talbot deserved the facts, yes; but none of the emotions that went along with them. She said coolly, "My mother died last winter. When I was going through her papers a month ago, I found a letter telling me I'd been adopted in England as a baby, twenty-six years ago. My twin sister had been adopted at the same time by a couple called Douglas and Clarissa Talbot, from Droverton in Cumbria.'' She paused, fighting the tightness in her throat. ''I hadn't known I was an adopted child. To cut a long story short, I decided to come to Droverton to meet Fiona. A long-overdue meeting, as I'm sure you'd agree.''

She seemed to have run out of words. She'd give her soul for a cup of hot, black coffee.

His voice laced with sarcasm, Douglas said, ''A charming story—and not a word of truth in it. Fiona was not adopted. So that's the end of it.''

''You can look at me, and deny every word I've told you? Fiona and I—we're identical twins. Of course she was adopted!''

Douglas leaned forward. ''Let me tell you something that I'm sure you already know. I have a considerable position in the business world and in society. A very considerable position.'' He gave the shabby little room a disparaging look. ''It would be greatly to your advantage to ally yourself with our family.''

''I couldn't care less—''

''But that's not all. My daughter is intimately associated with one of the richest men in England, an association that's moving toward marriage. You're telling me it's coincidence that at a time when an announcement is imminent Fiona's identical twin appears out of the blue? Come, come, Miss Marshall, you strain my credulity. And my patience.''

The black-haired stranger in the woods... ''Rich?'' Karyn faltered.

''Rafe Holden of Holden Enterprises. I'm sure even in the wilds of Canada you've heard of him.''

Karyn had certainly heard of the Holden chain of hotels, although she'd never stayed in one of them. Their cheapest rooms would have blown her budget for months. She said roundly, "I had no idea when I flew over here that Fiona was about to get engaged, let alone to whom. Nor would it have made any difference if I had."

"The kind of money Rafe Holden commands? I have no doubt it inspired your story from beginning to end." Douglas levered himself up from his chair. "You'll leave Droverton today, and you'll stay away from my daughter forever. Should you disobey me, there will be severe legal consequences—I will not tolerate any disturbance to my family's peace of mind, especially by a little upstart like you. Do I make myself clear?"

Karyn got to her feet, pink flags of fury in her cheeks. "I'm Fiona's twin sister. She was adopted by you and your wife twenty-six years ago. Don't you dare try to bully me."

His eyes looked as though they might pop out of his head. "Get out of Droverton today, Miss Marshall—you'll regret it if you don't."

He marched to the door, swung it open and slammed it shut behind him. Through the panels she could hear his footsteps clumping down the stairs. She went to the window that faced the street. A few minutes later, Douglas Talbot stalked over to a shiny silver Jaguar and barreled down the road in the direction of Willowbend.

So much for any fantasies she'd cherished of being warmly welcomed into the bosom of the family. How could Fiona stand having such a horrible father?

She stayed at the window, gazing down at the street. There was a cold lump in the vicinity of her heart. All along, she'd blithely assumed that Fiona knew she'd been adopted; that Fiona's parents hadn't chosen the same course as the Marshalls of keeping their child in ignorance. But

Fiona didn't know. As far as Fiona was concerned, Douglas and Clarissa were her only parents and there were no shadows around her birth.

Was she, Karyn, to be the one to tell Fiona the truth? She could remember as clearly as if it were yesterday how the discovery of her own adoption had shocked her to the core, causing her to look at her parents with new eyes. How could she expose Fiona to the same doubts and confusion?

She couldn't. Which meant she was barred from meeting Fiona now or ever.

Stay away from my daughter forever…

Lanced by pain, Karyn moved away from the window. Now that it had become totally impossible to approach her sister, she realized how much she'd been counting on meeting her, finding out what it was like to have an identical twin.

Both her own parents were dead, and she was an only child; she was alone in the world. What a cliché, Karyn thought with an unhappy twist to her lips. But how lonely those words made her feel; and how understandable that she'd come all the way from Prince Edward Island to Cumbria to find her sister.

She looked around the little room with sudden loathing. She couldn't stay here one more minute. If Willowbend was out of bounds, then she'd go somewhere else. Because, of course, it wasn't just Fiona who was on her mind.

Rafe, she thought. Rafe Holden. It was a name that suited him, that dark-eyed man who'd kissed her under the trees thinking she was Fiona; and to whom she'd responded mindlessly and with the total abandon of desire. Even now, she could remember the strength of his arms around her, the sensitivity with which he'd stroked her breast, the way he'd invited her to his bed.

Douglas Talbot had confirmed that Rafe and Fiona were lovers. Lovers who were soon to be married.

Shivering, Karyn paced up and down, the floorboards groaning underfoot. When she'd looked up Droverton and its environs on the Internet, she'd read about Holden Castle, an exclusive retreat west of the village. The man who'd kissed her owned it, along with dozens of other internationally-known luxury resorts.

He'd spoken to her so gently, thinking she was Fiona. He'd tried to soothe her fears, and he'd wanted her to enjoy his bed and his body. Tears filled Karyn's eyes. Steve had never cherished her in that way.

She clamped down viciously on thoughts of Steve; the only way she knew how to deal with those memories was to repress them. However, when she transferred her attention to her present predicament, Karyn felt just as unhappy. She had to leave Droverton for Fiona's sake, certainly. Rafe Holden was the other reason, equally pressing, that she must get away from here. She couldn't risk meeting him again. It would be too humiliating, too upsetting.

Her quest was over before it had begun.

Impulsively Karyn grabbed the little folder supplied by the inn and flipped through it. Picking up the antiquated phone, she dialed the number of the nearest car rental agency. To heck with her budget. She'd go nuts if she sat in this room all day.

Late that afternoon, Karyn was driving back along the narrow roads toward Droverton. She'd tramped the fells, rented a rowboat on one of the lakes, lunched in a pub and seen innumerable shaggy sheep. On the outskirts of Coverdale, she'd had a calorie-laden tea sitting on a balcony overlooking tree-clad hills and velvet-green fields neatly edged with stone. She felt, marginally, better.

She'd also made a decision. She was going to leave Droverton today. She had no other choice. She couldn't risk hurting Fiona in any way.

As she coasted down a hill on the approach to the village, she caught a glimpse of a rose-brick mansion tucked among the trees. Impetuously she pulled over onto the verge and got out of her car. Crossing the road, she leaned on the stone wall and gazed down at Willowbend.

It might as well have been on the other side of the world.

Another car was approaching. Studiously she kept her gaze trained on the view, doing her best to look like one more tourist admiring the scenery. But the other vehicle pulled up behind hers; as the engine was turned off, the distant bleating of sheep sounded very loud in the silence. Furious with the intruder, Karyn turned to see who was disturbing her privacy.

Rafe Holden was crossing the grassy verge toward her, his hands jammed in his pockets. It was the first time she'd seen him in daylight. Rapidly she skimmed his face with its broad cheekbones, strongly modeled jawline and hard-set mouth. His black hair was thick, glossy as a raven's wing; his dark eyes stormy.

He was taller than she remembered. Taller than Steve, she realized with an inward judder of her nerves; and more powerfully built. His whipcord trousers were snug to his hips, while his open-neck shirt revealed a physique wholly and disturbingly masculine. Would she ever forget that devastating kiss under the oak tree?

For a moment her gaze flicked to his hunter-green sports car. She didn't know much about cars, but she'd be willing to bet this particular one represented five years of her salary.

Somehow this gave her the courage to go on the offensive. She said coldly, "Why don't you get back in your car and drive straight to Willowbend? It's where you belong—and you're the last person in the world I want to see right now.''

''In that case, why did you station yourself on a public road overlooking Fiona's house?''

''I don't owe you any explanations!''

''That's where you're wrong,'' Rafe said with dangerous softness. ''I want to know who you are and what you're doing here—and I'm not leaving until you tell me.''

One of Steve's legacies to Karyn was a fear of large angry men. For Rafe Holden was angry, she was in no doubt about that. But they were standing in the open, and what could he do to her, short of bundling her into his car or tossing her over the wall? She retorted, ''I don't respond well to threats.''

''I don't like women who trespass on other people's property and run away without explaining. Why don't we start with your name?''

While he didn't look remotely like an ally, neither did he look at all like Douglas Talbot. Wasn't Rafe Holden her last chance to reach Fiona? Maybe Douglas had been lying and Fiona did know she was adopted; as Fiona's lover, Rafe was in a position to know the truth.

What did she have to lose? Nothing.

''My name is Karyn Marshall,'' she said. ''I'm from eastern Canada, a place called Heddingley in Prince Edward Island.''

''That explains the accent...you're a long way from home. What brought you here? And take your time, I'm in no rush.''

Trying to ignore the sarcasm in his voice, Karyn looked out over the peaceful valley. ''This all began when my mother died six months ago. Unexpectedly. It was a huge shock to me.''

Rafe stood still, watching every change of expression on her face. Her profile was Fiona's. But her hair clung like a gold helmet to her head, emphasizing the elegance of her cheekbones and the slender line of her throat. Her eyes were bluer than Fiona's. Or was it just that they were more direct?

She was slimmer than Fiona, he saw, as the breeze molded her flowered dress to her body; fiercely he quelled a flame of desire, and, almost hidden beneath it, a flicker of fear. He'd assumed, in the middle of the night, that daylight would bring with it a return to sanity, burying passion where it belonged. "What happened to your mother?" he asked brusquely.

"An aneurysm. She died instantly." Unconsciously Karyn was smoothing the rock beneath her fingers. "It took several months before I could bring myself to sort through her belongings. My father died ten years ago, and I have no brothers or sisters. So there was only me."

Her fingers were slender and ringless; delicate shadows lay in the hollows under her collarbone, while her face was thin, as though she had indeed been through some hard experiences. Hating himself for feasting on her like a starving man, Rafe forced himself to listen. "Four weeks ago," she was saying, "I found some papers in her jewelry box. Among them was a letter to be opened by me only in the event of her death." She bent her head, picking at a clump of moss with her nails, fighting the tightness in her chest. Then she looked full at him, all the blue of the sky shimmering in her eyes. "I have that letter with me now. I'd hoped to show it to the Talbots."

"What does the letter say?" Rafe asked noncommittally.

"My parents were both English. They met in Sheffield and married there—they loved each other very much, that much I've always known, and they wanted children. But after my mother had three miscarriages, they decided to adopt. I was only two weeks old when they were notified about me. My birth mother, so the letter said, was a single woman who'd refused to divulge my father's name and who later moved to Australia. She died in an accident in Sydney when I was just a year old.''

Again Karyn bent her head, wishing she didn't find this recital so painful. ''You can imagine how I felt,'' she said in a low voice. ''But there was more. The letter went on to say that I had a twin sister. Although my father had done his best to adopt both of us, another couple had put in a prior claim on my twin. Through a bureaucratic foul-up, my father was sent the adoption certificate for Fiona by mistake. Douglas and Clarissa Talbot, from Droverton in Cumbria—my mother had written down every detail she knew.'' She glanced up, noticing for the first time that Rafe's eyes weren't black, as she'd thought last night, but the darkest of blues. Like a lake at dusk, she thought, full of secrets. ''That's why I'm here, Mr. Holden. I came to meet my twin sister, Fiona.''

''So until a month ago, you knew none of this?''

There was an edge to his voice. Karyn flushed. ''That's right. The letter ended by describing my parents' mutual decision to keep the truth from me about the adoption.'' *We only wanted to spare you pain, darling, and we couldn't have loved you more had you been born to us,* her mother had written. *In all the ways that count, you are indeed our dearly beloved daughter.*

The words were inscribed on Karyn's memory; she'd remember them, she was sure, for the rest of her life. But they were too intimate to share with Rafe Holden. Clearing her throat, she went on, ''At first I was paralyzed by shock. I felt ungrounded, as though the world had rocked on its foundations and everything I'd taken for granted had been a lie. Then I got really angry that they'd never told me.'' She bit her lip. ''I don't know why I'm telling you this. I haven't told anyone. I couldn't at the time, it was too painful.''

The fragility of her wrists, the strain in her voice: Rafe was almost overwhelmed by the urge to take her in his arms and comfort her. Or was he fooling himself? Maybe all he really wanted to do was kiss her senseless.

Passion. He'd sworn off it years ago. So what was it about Karyn Marshall that drew him like an eagle to its mate?

Whatever it was, he resented it deeply.

He said with brutal honesty, ''I grew up in Droverton, and I've known Fiona all my life. If she'd been adopted, I'd have known.''

''You'd only have been a child at the time.''

''Seven years old. Old enough to know about village gossip. In all the years I've lived here there's never been a whisper of anything you've so touchingly described.''

''So you think I've made it all up,'' Karyn said, feeling cold creep into her bones.

''What else can I think?''

''And why would I bother spending money I can ill afford to cross the Atlantic on a fool's errand?''

''How would I know? Although if you're that strapped for cash, Willowbend would look pretty good.''

She wouldn't lose her temper. She wouldn't. Karyn said tightly, ''So, according to you, even the resemblance is coincidence.''

''What else can it be? Douglas might be a thoroughly unpleasant man at times, but one thing I know—he worships the ground Clarissa walks on and he'd never have been unfaithful to her. Nor she to him. So, yes, it's coincidence.''

"You're so logical, so cold-blooded," she cried. "Don't you have any room for emotion? I don't give a damn about money! All I want is to meet Fiona. My sister."

"When I kissed you last night," Rafe grated, "I wouldn't have called either one of us cold-blooded. Why didn't you tell me then who you were? You had the chance. Instead you played me like a fish on the hook, trying to insinuate yourself into Willowbend in any way you could. I hate being made a fool of. Particularly by a woman."

"I didn't do it on purpose! It just...happened."

Something in her pinched face infuriated him. "You expect me to believe that?" he rasped. "Let me tell you something else. Fiona and I have been friends for years. I'm a very rich man, Karyn Marshall, and you've just admitted your circumstances are straitened. So quit trying to convince me of the purity of your motives."

"You're despicable," Karyn seethed. "No better than Douglas, with whom I had a delightful interview this morning. Stay away or I'll put the legal sharks on you—that was the gist of his little speech."

Rafe's eyes narrowed. "Douglas came to see you? I didn't know that."

"Oh, yeah?" she said rudely.

How dare she compare him with Douglas? "I'm telling you the truth," Rafe said in a staccato voice.

"What do I care? For the last ten minutes you could have saved your breath—I've already decided to leave Droverton and stay away from Fiona, because she doesn't know she's adopted and it's not my job to tell her. To hurt her. But of course you're not going to believe me—I'm just a lying bitch who's after your bucks. You can keep them, Rafe Holden! I don't want them."

She looked so furious, so utterly convincing. But Fiona hadn't been adopted; he'd have known if she was. So Karyn

Marshall's whole story was fabrication from beginning to end. ''You belong on the stage,'' Rafe said coldly, ''you could make a fortune. Much as I hate to ally myself with Douglas, I'm going to repeat him. Leave here today and don't come back. Or you'll be sorry.''

''I can't get out of here soon enough.''

Karyn pushed herself away from the wall. But some rocks that had fallen from the wall were hidden under the grass; her sandal skidded on one of them. As she lurched sideways, Rafe automatically reached out to save her, one arm around her waist, the other steadying her shoulder.

For a moment that was frozen in time, Karyn sagged against him. The hard wall of his chest, the latent strength of his fingers, their burning heat through her dress: she was pierced by a knife of desire so sharp that she almost cried out. As though she couldn't help herself, she looked up, plunging into the dark depths of his eyes where she saw desire reflected, meeting her own, magnifying it. Briefly his arms tightened, so briefly that she wondered afterward if she'd imagined it. Then he thrust her away so hard that she staggered.

Trembling in every limb, Karyn fought for balance, all her distress and confusion rushing to the surface. ''Last night you could be forgiven, because you thought I was Fiona. But today you know I'm not. You wanted to kiss me a moment ago, didn't you? I know you did! How dare you kiss Fiona one day and me the next? As though we're interchangeable.''

Rafe stood still, her accusation throbbing in his brain. Karyn's body, so suddenly and unexpectedly in his arms, had struck him to the core. How could he deny it? How could he have prevented it? It had been elemental, instinctive, utterly beyond his control.

If he was going to marry Fiona, it was also totally against his principles.

He took refuge in anger. "Was that another of your clever little ploys—let's see if I can get him to kiss me again? What's next on the list?"

She paled, looking suddenly older than her years. "I'm not going to stand here and be insulted by you any longer. I'm only sorry for Fiona—her father's a bully, and you wouldn't recognize the truth if it was right under your nose. I never want to see either one of you again."

In a swirl of skirts she stumbled through the long grass, crushing wildflowers underfoot. After glancing both ways, she ran across the road, opened the door of her car and got in. Although her fingers were shaking, she finally got the key in the ignition. Dirt grinding from her tires, she drove away; and the whole time was aware of Rafe Holden standing like a statue by the wall. Making no move to stop her.

Rafe watched her go, his blood pounding in his ears. Years ago, Celine had been unfaithful to him, destroying his passion, his trust and his love as carelessly as if he'd meant nothing to her. Less than nothing. Today Karyn Marshall had accused him of infidelity toward Fiona. And wasn't it true? He was pulled toward Karyn as inexorably as the moon pulled the tides.

He had to find out if she'd been lying to him from the first moment he'd laid eyes on her, or if she'd been telling him the truth. He had to.

He'd go out of his mind if he didn't.

CHAPTER THREE

WHEN Karyn reached the inn, she parked her car, tied a headscarf over her hair and jammed on dark glasses. Then she hurried inside. The landlord was standing behind the counter in a wrinkled green shirt. He said, not bothering to hide his sneer, "Ah, Miss Marshall. I'm glad you're back. I will, unfortunately, be needing your room tonight for other guests. Would you settle up now?"

"That would give me great pleasure," she said, snapping her credit card on the counter. When he handed her the slip, it also gave her pleasure to put a long slash through the space for the tip. Then she looked up. "You can phone Mr. Talbot now and tell him I've left," she said sweetly. "Goodbye."

Ten minutes later she was driving out of the quadrangle behind the inn. She had no idea where she was going. Nor, at the moment, did she care.

For the last time she wound along the narrow road through Droverton, past the little shops and the stone cottages with their beautiful gardens. A few minutes later she passed the driveway to Willowbend.

Her throat tight, her eyes aching with unshed tears, Karyn drove on. It was early evening, the golden light a mockery to all her hopes, her sister receding with every turn in the road. Although, deep in her heart, she knew she was doing the right thing, that she couldn't have lived with herself had she done otherwise, she only wished it didn't hurt so abominably.

Then she saw, to her right, a layby tucked under the trees. Quickly she pulled over and got out. Her eyes sharpened. A little path led down the slope. After changing from sandals to walking shoes, Karyn locked the car and set off down the path.

If she walked for an hour or so, she'd feel better.

She took off her dark glasses and thrust her headscarf in the pocket of her dress. No more need for disguises. No need to hide. Just the distant chuckle of a woodland stream and her own thoughts.

Ten minutes later, the woods opened out in one of the vistas characteristic of this northern countryside: gentle hills blending into granite crags that faded blue into the distance. Always, somewhere, there was the glitter of water.

The landscape called to her, beckoning, almost as though she belonged here.

Not a train of thought she wanted to follow.

Karyn started climbing, feeling the pull on her leg muscles. When she came to the crest of the hill with its screen of gold-starred gorse and piled boulders, she stood still, her eyes widening in shock. Below her, edged by a tumble of rocks and the lazy curve of a river, were the battlements of a castle. Even from here she could see the formal gardens that surrounded the castle, the bright turquoise of a large rectangular pool, and lawns so green they made her eyes ache.

Holden Castle, she thought. Ancestral home of Rafe Holden.

As though she couldn't help herself, her gaze was dragged farther westward. Nestled in open fields edged with trees was a huge two-story stone house with south-facing wings, a glassed solarium and, again, the gleam of an outdoor pool. Its slate roofs were dark as shadows, its outbuildings surrounded by white-painted fencing. For all its civilized accoutrements, the house faced the fells and tarns, the rocky crags of the moor, and was perfectly suited to the wildness of its surroundings.

She squinted into the dying sun. Wasn't that a dark green sports car parked in the courtyard?

Rafe's car. The house must be his, too. A house so beautiful it made Karyn's heart ache. A house Fiona must know inside and out; she'd be mistress of it when she and Rafe married.

Into Karyn's mind came an image of the little clapboard house her mother had left her, where Karyn had grown up. The comparison was laughable.

Except she didn't feel like laughing.

Abruptly Karyn tensed. From her left, approaching fast, she heard the clump of hooves on the grass. Instinctively she ducked behind the line of boulders and gorse. The hooves slowed. A woman's voice said softly, ''Well done, Sasha. What a glorious sunset.''

With painstaking care Karyn peered between the stiff green branches. Horse and rider were perhaps thirty feet below her; the Arabian mare was tossing her head so the bridle jingled as the woman looked out over the peaceful valley. She was slim, clad in well-fitting jodphurs, a white shirt and a black hard hat. A thick coil of blond hair was pinned at her nape.

When she turned her head to the east, toward Willowbend, Karyn saw, as though in a mirror, her own profile with its straight nose and high cheekbones.

Hadn't she known, from the moment she first heard the sound of hooves, that the rider would be Fiona?

Her heart was thumping so hard in her breast that she was afraid Fiona would hear it. She sank lower behind the bushes, knees trembling from the strain. So near and yet so far. So unutterably far.

Fiona said cheerfully, ''We'd better get going, Sash. Mother's invited that dreadful old snob, Emily Fairweather, in for drinks and I'm expected to put in an appearance. Let's go down the hill and have a good gallop through Fenton's field—we'll jump the wall, how about it?''

Sasha blew through her nostrils, and as Karyn risked another glance, Fiona squeezed her knees and the horse trotted down the hillside. Within a couple of minutes horse and rider were out of sight. To her dismay Karyn realized she was weeping, a flood of silent tears streaming down her cheeks. She'd seen her sister, her twin. That one glimpse had to be enough for the rest of her life.

She cried for a long time, until she had no tears left. Then, blowing her nose and wiping her wet cheeks, she stood up. As though she couldn't help herself, her eyes were drawn once more to the stone house on Rafe's estate. In its mixture of the sophisticated and the untamed, wasn't it just like the man himself?

A man she'd never see again.

She started tramping back the way she'd come. Fiona, she could only assume, had been visiting Rafe…and why not?

They'd probably been in bed together.

She'd been very quick to accuse Rafe of infidelity toward Fiona. But hadn't she, Karyn, betrayed her sister as well, first in that incendiary kiss by the gardens of Willowbend, and then again this afternoon in that wild leap of her blood when she'd stumbled into Rafe's arms by the wall? How could she have responded with such passionate intensity to a man who was her sister's lover?

It was unforgivable. The only way for her to make amends was to vanish from both their lives.

Her steps quickened. At least she'd seen Fiona, Karyn thought stoutly. Once only, and all too briefly, but she'd been granted that much. In time, she was sure, she would be grateful for that small crumb of comfort.

The trees welcomed her into their embrace, and her vehicle was exactly where she'd left it. She climbed in, checked for other cars and pulled out onto the road.

By eight o'clock the next morning, Rafe was on the phone to one of his assistants in the London head office. "Vic? I want you to do something for me. Fast. Ready?"

Vic was from Manhattan and knew all about *fast*. "Right on," he said agreeably, focusing so he wouldn't miss the smallest detail. He liked working for Rafe Holden. Sure, the man was both demanding and exacting. But he was also fair, he didn't stand on ceremony and he paid extraordinarily well.

"This is confidential," Rafe added in a clipped voice.

"Understood."

"I want a thorough investigation on the following person, and I want results by the end of the day. Pay for the top people. Got that?"

"Yep. Go ahead."

"Karyn Marshall." Quickly Rafe gave the particulars of her rented car. "Find out where she's spending the night tonight and have her followed. I also want you to investigate a possible adoption twenty-six years ago of identical twins..." Speaking with crisp precision, Rafe gave every detail he'd learned from Karyn, along with the relevant information about the Talbots. He finished with the name of Karyn's hometown in Prince Edward Island. "Check how she earns her living, her marital status, anything at all."

Vic said imperturbably, "I'll set it in motion right away, and e-mail you as soon as anything turns up."

"Thanks, Vic."

Rafe put the phone down. He'd done it. Rightly or wrongly, he was going to find out whether Karyn had been telling him the truth, a partial truth, or a pack of lies. Maybe then he could put her out of his mind and get on with his life.

Running upstairs, he showered and shaved; he didn't look that great, he thought dispassionately, staring at himself in the mirror. Two sleepless nights in a row were taking their toll.

Had a chance meeting with a blond, blue-eyed woman made any thoughts of proposing to Fiona an utter impossibility?

Out of control, he thought savagely. That's how he felt. As though the course he'd been mapping for his life had been totally derailed. Was he wrong to want a peaceful domestic life? To opt for a well-marked track rather than the crags and peaks of passion?

Passion, betrayed, had ripped him apart.

Marriage to Fiona would never do that.

It was Douglas who'd put the idea of marriage in his head, five days ago in the oak-paneled study at Stoneriggs. Douglas wanted Rafe to rescue him from some ill-considered investments, that information had come out right away. But he also wanted Rafe to marry Fiona. How had he put it?

''You owe me, old man. Nothing Clarissa and I would like better than to welcome you into the family.''

''Owe you?'' Rafe repeated sharply.

''Remember when you turned twenty? Your mother gave you enough money that you could buy your first three properties. Get your start. She told you the money was left to her, an old great-uncle who'd died in the highlands of Scotland.'' Douglas gave a hearty laugh. ''Balderdash! I loaned her the money. I had you taped as someone who'd rise to the top, and I was right. So now I'm calling in the loan, Rafe. I want you to marry Fiona."

"I can't believe the money came from you!"

"Just ask your mother," Douglas said smugly.

"You can be sure I will."

"So what's your answer, Rafe?"

"You're not getting one right now," Rafe said, steel in his voice. "I'll need a month to think about it. In the meantime, you're not to say a word to anyone—least of all Fiona—or I won't touch your debts. Is that clear?"

With bad grace Douglas agreed, and took his leave. Rafe then drove as fast as he could to the castle. "Darling, your father and I would have done anything to get you away from here," Joan Holden said. "Don't you remember what it was like the whole time you were growing up? Death duties to the eyeballs and the walls falling down around us."

Rafe remembered all too well. In a twisted way he did owe Douglas a debt of gratitude: those first three properties had started him on the road to fortune. But Douglas hadn't loaned the money all those years ago out of the goodness of his heart. Oh, no. Douglas desperately wanted an alliance with Holden blue blood, and had gambled on Rafe as the means to achieve this.

Rafe loathed the prospect of being manipulated like a chess piece by a player as crass as Douglas. But the more he thought about it, the more he realized how ready he was to settle down, and how deeply he wanted to avoid the intensity of emotion Celine had evoked in him. He'd known Fiona all his life, and would have trusted her with his life. Besides, Fiona would be all too happy to settle at Stoneriggs, for, like himself, she loved the hills and dales of his estate.

He'd been rather pleased with these conclusions. But

then he'd met Karyn, and had discovered that the passion he'd thought he'd outgrown was very much alive.

One kiss was all it had taken.

The phone rang at five past eleven that night in Rafe's study. He barked his name into the receiver.

Picking up on his boss's tone immediately, Vic said, "I've sent you an e-mail filling in the details. The rundown's like this. Karyn Marshall left Droverton late yesterday and booked into the Warm Hearts Bed and Breakfast in Hart's Run for two nights. She and Fiona Talbot are identical twins, adopted at age two weeks by the Marshalls and the Talbots respectively. Karyn's employed as a veterinarian at the Heddingley Clinic near Charlottetown, Prince Edward Island. Her husband, Steven Patterson, died a year ago. No children from the marriage." Vic paused. "You hadn't authorized investigation of peripheral people, so we didn't follow up on the husband."

Husband... his head reeling, Rafe said, "That's fine. I'll check the e-mail and get back to you if I have any questions. Good job, Vic, thanks."

The e-mail described Karyn's childhood, schooling, university degrees, marriage and career. Facts, facts and more facts. One of particular interest was that twenty-seven years ago Douglas had taken his wife to Italy for a year; when they returned to Droverton via London, they'd brought a baby with them. So that, thought Rafe, was how they'd avoided village gossip.

He got up from his chair and walked over to the windows that overlooked the crags he'd climbed as a boy. The main points in Vic's report he'd already known, because Karyn had told them to him. She hadn't lied. She'd told the truth from beginning to end.

Although not the whole truth. She hadn't said anything

about being widowed. As clearly as if she were standing in front of him, he could remember her slim, ringless fingers.

Either way, he'd accused her of social climbing, avarice and deceit. Well done, Rafe. You're going to have to work damn hard to jam your foot any further down your throat. What are you planning for an encore?

Wasn't that the issue? What *was* he going to do for an encore? He had two choices. Delete the e-mail, pay the bill for the investigators and forget Karyn Marshall existed. Or get in touch with her and bring her and Fiona together.

He started pacing up and down the room, his emotions roiling. The easy course was to do nothing. Let the secrets of many years remain secrets. Karyn had already left Droverton and would—he knew in his heart—stay away. She wouldn't risk hurting Fiona as she had been hurt by her own parents' deception. She'd told him that, her blue eyes meeting his unflinchingly. And hadn't he just been given proof that every word she'd spoken had been trustworthy?

If he took the easy way out, he'd never have to see Karyn again. The fierce attraction she'd exerted on him simply by existing would fade from his memory and from his body, becoming part of the past, a temporary madness.

Eclipsed by his marriage to her sister?

Fiona. Even as a boy, Rafe had understood that the heart of Fiona's rich and comfortable life harbored an acute loneliness. She had no brothers and sisters, and her parents, while they loved her, were controlling and manipulative in ways sweet-natured Fiona was only rarely aware of. Was it fair to keep her in ignorance of her sister's existence?

Karyn, although she was Fiona's identical twin, had been differently molded. She wasn't rich: when she'd sold the house that had been in her dead husband's name, she'd used the money to pay off a substantial student loan. Which brought Rafe back to the fact he'd been trying to avoid. Karyn had loved a man enough to marry him, and had suffered from his death. When she'd been standing by the wall in the sunlight, Rafe had been achingly aware of the character in her face, her features honed by experiences he'd chosen to disparage. Now he had some idea of what those experiences had been.

Fiona might learn what she herself was capable of from the woman who was her identical twin. Who better as a teacher? And was it up to him to prevent this from happening?

He had that power of prevention. He was a man used to wielding power. He could, single-handedly, keep the two sisters apart for the rest of their days.

Abruptly Rafe grabbed a jacket from the cupboard and opened the French doors to the stone patio. Hands thrust in his pockets, he set off through the garden toward the woods. He always thought better outdoors.

Temporary madness. That's what he'd called it and that's all it was, that kiss in the woods at dusk, that streak of lust when Karyn had fallen into his arms by the wall. He'd get over it.

From his left, deep in the trees, an owl hooted, a wild, plaintive cry that shivered along his nerves. Be honest, Rafe, he told himself caustically. The attraction went deeper than that. She'd felt it, too. Unarguably. Blood to blood and bone to bone.

Flesh to flesh.

How could he marry Fiona when he felt this overwhelming attraction toward a woman he hadn't known existed two days ago?

One thing at a time. His primary decision right now was whether he should bring the two sisters together. Because Karyn, he suspected, wouldn't hang around the area very long.

What was he going to do?

At seven the following evening, Rafe was navigating the narrow streets of Hart's Run, forty miles from Droverton. Fiona was sitting beside him in his adored green Ferrari. She said lightly, "You're being very mysterious, Rafe."

"There's someone I want you to meet, that's all," he said just as casually. Although he didn't feel casual. He felt as though he was playing God. A highly uncomfortable role and not one he aspired to.

"But who?"

"You'll see." He swung into the parking lot of the Hart Inn, where, so one of the investigators had informed him earlier today, Karyn had made a dinner reservation. Turning to face Fiona, he said, "Just keep an open mind, that's all. Promise?"

"*Very* mysterious." She gave him her sweet smile. "You know I'd promise you anything."

When he led Fiona into the dining room, Rafe saw Karyn immediately. His heart gave a great thud in his chest. Schooling his features to immobility, he took Fiona by the hand and threaded through the tables. Karyn was reading the menu. Then, as though she felt the pull of his gaze, she looked up, dropped the menu on the cloth and gaped at him. "Rafe?" she croaked.

He said easily, "I've brought someone to meet you," and stood aside so Karyn could see Fiona.

Shaken to the core, Karyn felt the color drain from her cheeks. Enough of a shock to see Rafe. But to discover in the space of seconds that he was accompanied by Fiona...she gripped the edge of the table, her knuckles white with strain, and said raggedly, ''Hello…won't you both sit down?''

Fiona sank into the nearest chair, her eyes glued to Karyn's face. ''I'd heard gossip in the village about a woman who resembled me,'' she said dazedly. ''We're the image of each other—it's amazing!'' She turned to Rafe. ''Why didn't you tell me?''

Karyn's brain stumbled into action. So Fiona didn't know who she was. Rafe hadn't told her.

To her infinite relief the waiter appeared on the scene. ''Will the gentleman and the lady be joining you, madam?''

''Er—yes,'' Karyn faltered. ''At least, I hope so.''

''I wouldn't leave for worlds,'' Fiona said, smiling at the waiter as he put two more menus on the table. When he'd gone, she turned that smile on Karyn. ''You must tell me who you are—I don't even know your name.''

One step at a time. ''Karyn Marshall. My home's in Prince Edward Island on the east coast of Canada.''

''We can't possibly be related then,'' Fiona said. ''Yet we could be sisters, we look so much alike.''

In desperation Karyn sent Rafe a hunted look. He was sitting across from her, the light from the window delineating his strongly carved features. But not penetrating his eyes, she thought with an inward shiver. They were like rooms locked against her. He said flatly, ''Fiona, I want you to listen to me. Remember what I said in the car, about keeping an open mind?''

Fiona's smile faded. ''I don't understand…''

''There's no easy way to tell you. You and Karyn—you look alike because you *are* sisters. Twin sisters.''

As Karyn's jaw dropped that he could admit to a truth he'd so bitterly denied, Fiona frowned in puzzlement. ''How can we be?'' she said. ''That's impossible.''

''You were adopted,'' Rafe said bluntly. ''You and

Karyn have the same birth mother. Douglas and Clarissa didn't tell you they'd adopted you, and Karyn didn't find out she'd been adopted until recently, after her mother died. That's why she came here—to find you."

There, he thought. He'd done it. He'd altered, irrevocably and in a few words, the lives of several people.

"Adopted? You're saying I'm *adopted?*"

"That's right," Rafe said steadily, taking her hand in his and raising it to his cheek in a gesture that seemed to Karyn, distraught though she was, more like comfort between friends than intimacy between lovers. She shoved the thought away, concentrating on what Rafe was saying. "I know this is a huge shock to you, Fiona. But I didn't feel I could keep the truth from you, or rob you of your sister's presence in your life."

Tears flooded Karyn's eyes; she blinked them back as Rafe went on, "All these years your parents have kept you from knowing the truth. And I have to be honest—when I first talked to Karyn, I didn't believe her story any more than your father did."

Fiona looked straight at Karyn. "You've met my father?"

"He came to see me at the inn in Droverton, yes."

Rafe said grimly, "He warned Karyn off. Told her to vanish and threatened her with severe repercussions if she didn't. Regrettably, I did the same thing."

Fiona was sitting like a woman stunned. Karyn whispered, "Rafe, whatever made you change your mind?"

"I had you investigated, and found out that every word you'd said was true."

As she winced, Fiona cried, "It can't be true! My parents wouldn't have deceived me—keeping me in the dark about my real roots. They couldn't be so cruel!"

Rafe grimaced. Still gripping her hand in his, he said

gently, "I'm afraid they did keep the truth from you. Maybe from the best of motives, who knows?"

She was glaring at him almost as though she hated him; then transferred that glare to Karyn. "I don't believe a word you've said to me, either one of you. If this is your idea of a joke, Rafe, I don't think it's remotely funny. I'm not—"

"Fiona, hiding your head in the sand—"

"I'm not sitting here listening to the two of you lie about my parents!" She shot Karyn a furious glance. "As far as I'm concerned you can go back to Canada on the first plane and stay there. I never want to see you again!"

She thrust her chair back, surged to her feet and hurried off between the tables. The conversation in their vicinity, which had dropped to a fascinated hush, hurriedly picked up.

"Hell and damnation," Rafe muttered. Then he, too, got to his feet. Without so much as a backward glance at Karyn, he followed Fiona out of the dining room.

Like magic, the waiter reappeared. "Is there a problem, madam?" he said politely.

Oh, no, Karyn thought hysterically, no problem. I've just been responsible for wrecking my sister's peace of mind and destroying all her illusions, that's all. "I'll be dining alone after all," she said. "Would you bring me a carafe of your house wine, please?"

"Certainly, madam."

He disappeared. Karyn stared out the window at the pretty garden that edged the river, while pain, dismay and, undeniably, gratitude battled for supremacy in her breast. Rafe had done his best to bring her and Fiona together; for that, she was truly thankful. However, despite his efforts, Fiona had repudiated her; and how that hurt.

The waiter poured her a glass of wine. She took the first sip, still gazing out at the peaceful scene on the other side of the glass. There was another layer to her pain. Seeing Rafe and Fiona together had also hurt. Hurt horribly, in a way she couldn't possibly justify. Naturally, Rafe had gone after Fiona rather than staying and comforting herself. His allegiance was to Fiona: they were lovers. What right did she, Karyn, have to be hurt?

Yet had she entirely misread their body language? Not once had she gained any sense of sexual intimacy between them, of the small, significant signals that bespeak the privacy of the bedroom and the sharing of a mutual passion.

Or was she fooling herself? Maybe she didn't want to see those signals.

Because she was jealous? Karyn took another sip of wine, briefly closing her eyes. It would have been far better if she'd left Cumbria two days ago, after that one glimpse of Fiona riding her Arabian mare on the grassy slopes near Willowbend.

Better, too, never to have seen Rafe again.

CHAPTER FOUR

RIGHT after breakfast the next day, Karyn set off on foot down the main street of Hart's Run, a narrow, cobbled street lined with charming boutiques hung with baskets of fuchsias and geraniums. Yesterday she'd noticed a little wool shop there. When she was upset, knitting was very good therapy, although the results were unpredictable. She might be a dab hand at spaying cats, but she couldn't knit for beans.

Her eyes were scratchy from lack of sleep and her limbs felt heavy. She'd stayed in her room all evening, hoping against hope that either Rafe or Fiona might get in touch; but the phone had remained distressingly silent. Once she'd bought the wool, she was going back to her room, phoning the airline and heading south. She wanted to go home, to the known and the familiar.

If she was running away, too bad.

In the wool shop Karyn found a delightful shade of pink mohair and a pattern that appealed to her. She left the shop and walked back toward the inn. It was raining, a fine, misty rain that fell softly on her face, gathering in drops on her cheeks like tears. But she wasn't going to cry. Not for Rafe and not for Fiona. She was going home instead.

As she approached the bed and breakfast, a green sports car drew up alongside her. To her utter consternation Rafe got out, followed by Fiona. The bag of wool slipped from her fingers and plopped into a puddle.

Rafe bent down and fished it out of the puddle. ''Good

thing someone invented plastic bags,'' he said with a crooked grin.

Quite rationally, Karen decided to lose her temper. In a gush of adrenaline she grabbed for the bag. ''Thank you,'' she snapped insincerely. ''Now why don't the two of you get lost? You'll be delighted to know I'm getting on the first available flight home and neither one of you will ever see me again. Rafe, give me the damned wool!''

He shook droplets of dirty water from the bag and passed it to her, his fingers lingering briefly on hers. ''Fiona has something to say to you.''

The touch of his lean fingers had surged through Karyn's body like a river in full spate. It did nothing to calm her. ''I'm not having a conversation with either one of you in the middle of the sidewalk. Or anywhere else. Too much was said last night and as far as I'm concerned, that's it.''

Fiona grabbed her by the wrist. ''Don't go! Please, Karyn, don't go...''

Karyn... To hear her own name in her sister's voice brought sudden tears to Karyn's eyes. She brushed them away. ''Fiona, I can't take any more of this, don't you see? If you don't believe a word I—''

''Rafe told me all about you on the way home yesterday. How you really were my sister and what he'd found out about you in the investigation.''

''He had no right to—''

''But I had to see my parents before I could take it all in. I had a terrible fight with them last night. I asked them if I was adopted and told them I'd met you. They denied everything, they yelled and screamed at me, it was awful. You were an imposter, they said, I wasn't ever to see you again. They went on and on until I thought I'd be sick.'' She shuddered. ''They were so upset, so adamant, that I knew they were lying. I just knew it. So I went over to

Rafe's first thing this morning and begged him to help me find you again.''

''Oh,'' said Karyn.

''I don't blame you for being angry,'' Fiona whispered.

''I'm not angry anymore,'' Karyn said truthfully, pushing down a wild hope that frightened her with its intensity.

''You see, I love animals, too. You're a vet and I volunteer at the local animal shelter—that's the only thing that's ever made me defy my parents. Can you sing?''

Karyn blinked. ''Not a note.''

''Can you paint or sculpt?''

''Nope. Hopeless.'' Karyn indicated the bag of wool. ''Can't knit, either. Although I keep trying.''

''Neither can I.'' Fiona gave her a watery smile. ''We're very much alike—and I don't just mean looks. We really are twins!''

''You won't change your mind?'' Karyn faltered.

''Oh, no. I know you're my sister.'' Impetuously Fiona flung her arms around Karyn. ''Oh, Karyn,'' she sobbed, ''I have a twin, I'm not alone anymore. I'm so happy, I can't tell you how happy I am—why am I crying?''

Tears were streaming down Karyn's face, too. She hugged Fiona as hard as she could, and within her the terrible loneliness that had been the legacy of her mother's death eased for the first time. ''I'm happy, too,'' she mumbled. ''I'm so glad we've found each other.''

More moved than he cared to admit, Rafe looked away. Such emotion was private, even though he was the one who'd brought it about.

How could he possibly regret what he'd done? Yet his whole body was filled with foreboding. From now on, Karyn would—inevitably—become part of his life.

Fiona had been astonishingly brave to have withstood the combined rage of Douglas and Clarissa last night. She'd need his support on the home front more than ever now. As a friend, certainly; although if she could claim him as her fiancé, that would give her a lot more clout. He winced inwardly, because as he watched the two sisters locked in each other's arms, it was to Karyn that his gaze was drawn.

When Karyn and Fiona eventually disentangled themselves, scrubbing at their wet cheeks, he said curtly, "You know, it might be as well if you both had DNA tests. That way you can show your parents irrefutable proof, Fiona. It could help get them off your back."

"Good idea," Karyn said warmly.

Fiona gaped at her. "You mean you would?"

"Of course." Karyn spoke the simple truth. "I'd do anything for you, Fiona."

More tears spilled from Fiona's spectacular blue eyes. Which were, Karyn thought wryly, just like her own. She added, "We'll do it today, if you like."

"Why not?" Fiona said recklessly. She gave Karyn the full benefit of her smile. "I never knew I could be this brave. I actually yelled at my mother, can you believe it?"

"I'd love to have been a fly on the wall," Rafe said.

"For once, I didn't need you there—I managed fine on my own," Fiona said. "Although I'm sure I'll need your help when I go home today. Mother will have had time to replenish her arsenal, and as for Dad—" She gave a small shudder.

"I'll look after your father," Rafe announced.

Fiona looked back at Karyn. "If you can become a vet, I can do five days a week at the shelter."

Karyn laughed. "If you can stand up to your parents, I can ask for a raise when I get home."

"If you can ask for a raise, I can be late for dinner."

They laced their arms together, giggling like two little girls. Rafe said dryly, "I'm not sure the world's ready for you two. Let's go find some good strong coffee, how about it?''

Karyn stood tall, knowing there was something she had to say. Her blue eyes steady, she said quietly, ''Rafe, I can't thank you enough for what you've done. If it hadn't been for you, Fiona and I would never have found each other.''

A lump in his throat, Rafe said huskily, ''My pleasure.''

''It's true,'' Fiona quavered, and threw herself into his arms. ''Thank you, thank you. I owe you so much already, and now this as well...you're so good to me, Rafe.''

Karyn's nails dug into her palms as Rafe's arms went around Fiona's waist; although again she had that illusory sense that the embrace was compounded more of companionship and gratitude than anything as basic as sex. But what did it matter? Either way, Fiona was in Rafe's arms, where she belonged. Where Karyn never would. She looked away, her happiness stabbed by a shaft of pain so strong it appalled her. In a flash the implications of the last few minutes passed before her eyes. Rafe would be a part of her life from now on. Her sister's lover. Maybe even her sister's husband. Always there. Always out of reach.

So what, she thought fiercely. Rafe was nothing to her. Nothing. Nor was she going to allow him to ruin her newfound joy. Instead she should be happy for Fiona that she had such a strong protector in Rafe.

Steeling herself, she watched as Rafe's hold loosened and Fiona stepped back. She *was* happy for Fiona. Of course she was.

Half an hour later, sitting at a table that overlooked a small mist-wreathed lake, Karyn's resolve to be happy was severely tested. As they drank pungent Colombian coffee accompanied by sinfully rich pastries, Fiona said artlessly, ''Where do we go from here? Literally, I mean.''

"Not to the inn in Droverton," Karyn said. "I royally insulted the landlord before I left."

"I can't expose you to my parents right now," Fiona said. "Even if they'd agree to have you at Willowbend, which I doubt."

"Easy," Rafe drawled. "The two of you can stay at Stoneriggs."

"Wonderful!" Fiona exclaimed.

"No way," Karyn gasped.

"You can have adjoining rooms in the east wing. Lots of horses to ride, Karyn, if that interests you."

She loved to ride. "I scarcely know you, Rafe. I couldn't possibly come and stay with you." Expose herself to Rafe and Fiona's love affair at close hand? Every nerve in her body screamed revolt.

"I could stable Sasha at Stoneriggs," Fiona said eagerly. "Can you ride, Karyn?"

"Yes," Karyn said grudgingly. "But—"

"Then that's settled," Fiona said. "If we went right now, I could collect Sasha and we could ride after lunch. We can swim in the pool every day, too. Oh, Karyn, it'll be such fun!"

Karyn bit her lip. Short of stamping her feet and throwing a tantrum, she was trapped. "Just as long as you know I'll have to go home in a few days," she said.

"All the more reason to enjoy today," Fiona said, and drained her coffee.

Stoneriggs, close up, took Karyn's breath away. The house, its stonework dampened by mist, was so imposing, so exquisitely proportioned; the informal gardens such a riot of color and scent. The pool, the tennis courts, the moss-green lawns, all surrounded by the wildness of the fells: overwhelmed, she said softly, "It's incredibly beautiful, Rafe."

"The favorite of all my houses," he said casually. "I'm here whenever I can be."

Because of the house? Or because of Fiona? Quelling a shaft of pain, Karyn said, "I can see why."

He then took them on a tour of the stables, where Karyn was reduced to an entranced silence. She walked into stall after stall, rubbing flanks glossy with health, murmuring endearments to each and every thoroughbred: mare, stallion and gelding; bay, chestnut and palomino. Wistfully she said, "You've got the horses in Heddingley beat by a country mile."

"Fiona will help you pick your mount," Rafe replied, his eyes trained on her enchanted face. "Why don't we go inside so you can change? Then I'll drive Fiona over to Willowbend to get Sasha."

So he could be alone with Fiona for a few minutes. Karyn said brightly, "That sounds like a great idea."

Inside, Rafe had opted for simplicity of décor. Off-white paint, the clean lines of Finnish and Swedish furniture, and polished oak parquet scattered with richly hued Persian carpets that even to Karyn's uneducated eye screamed money. The few pieces of art had obviously been chosen with great care.

Of all this, Fiona would be mistress.

Feeling suddenly exhausted, craving solitude, she gripped the banister as she climbed the long curve of staircase to the second floor. Rafe said sharply, "Are you all right, Karyn?"

Hating him for seeing too much, she muttered, "Too much emotion, I guess."

Fiona put an arm around her sister. "Why don't you lie down for a few minutes? Rafe and I will take our time…it doesn't matter if we don't go riding until later. The mist's supposed to clear sometime this afternoon.''

So within minutes Karyn was alone in her bedroom. As Rafe closed the door, her shoulders sagged with relief. She hadn't anticipated the degree of strain it would cause her to be in his presence, on his home territory. Yet Stoneriggs was the logical place for her to stay.

She must make the best of it. Focus on Fiona, not Rafe.

Her bedroom was painted a soft apricot, with a thick-piled cream-colored carpet, silk draperies and delicate floral prints on the walls. The tall windows overlooked the rose garden; a frilly bouquet of peonies had been placed by the big bed. In which, of course, she would sleep alone.

Where would Fiona sleep? Next door? Or with Rafe?

Don't go there, she scolded herself, throwing her jodphurs and shirt on the pretty armchair. Then she fell onto the bed and within moments was asleep.

A sleep that twelve hours later Karyn regretted.

It was now midnight. The mist had cleared; stars jittered in the sky and her body ached with tiredness. She and Fiona had had a wonderful ride among the crags of the moor; they'd swum in the pool, eaten gourmet French cuisine in the informal dining room that led onto a stone patio, and picked armloads of roses and honeysuckle for the lounge that they shared on the second floor. They'd laughed a lot and talked. Talked endlessly, trying to catch up on twenty-six lost years.

Every moment they spent together confirmed the unconscious bonds of twinship and their growing ease with each other, and for this Karyn was deeply grateful. She was also grateful for Rafe's tact: most of the day he'd absented himself, as though he realized how important it was that the two sisters be alone to explore their new relationship.

And now she couldn't go to sleep. Restlessly Karyn

roamed up and down, her feet sinking into the carpet. Through the wall she could hear the small sounds of Fiona having a shower, then moving around her bedroom. A few moments later something dropped on the bathroom tiles. Karyn's nerves fluttered. She stopped dead beside her bed, her ears straining. Wasn't that the opening and closing of a door?

Feeling like a spy, yet unable to help herself, Karyn waited a few seconds, then very softly opened her own door. Fiona, in a long blue gown, was gliding down the hall. As Karyn watched, she turned the corner and disappeared.

Swiftly Karyn retreated. Why, oh why, couldn't she have fallen asleep at eleven, when she and Fiona had said an emotional good-night out in the hallway? But no, she'd had to stay awake, and be given incontrovertible proof that Fiona and Rafe were lovers. No matter that their body language said otherwise. No matter that Rafe desired her, Karyn. Fiona was even now in Rafe's bedroom, in his arms.

For the second time that day, tears flooded Karyn's eyes. Leaning against the wall, she fought them back. She had to accept the hard truth of her sister's relationship with Rafe. She had no other choice.

It was only Fiona who was important here, she thought fiercely. Not Rafe. She simply couldn't afford to let Rafe ruin the growing bond between herself and her sister.

Oddly enough, as the days passed, Karyn was helped in this resolve by Rafe. He flew to Paris one day, to Prague another. He rarely rode with them, and never joined them in the pool, pleading the pressures of work. At mealtimes, he was a charming, witty conversationalist who might just as well have been a chance acquaintance.

Karyn should have been happy with this state of affairs. Instead, against all logic, she was infuriated.

On the fifth evening, she and Fiona couldn't resist the flushed evening sky and went for a ride on the moors after dinner. When they got back, Karyn collapsed into one of the chairs on the patio, running her fingers through her tousled curls. ''That was wonderful.''

Fiona sat down beside her. Taking off her hard hat, she said with unusual hesitancy, ''Karyn, there's something I've been wanting to ask you...''

''Go ahead.''

''We've talked about so much—but not about your husband. You never even mention his name.''

Karyn said shortly, ''I don't like talking about him.''

''I know it was only a year ago that he died...you must still miss him dreadfully.''

As Karyn leaned over to rub dust from her riding boots, mumbling an indistinct reply, Fiona persisted, ''What did he look like? Was he a vet, too?''

''He was an accountant with an international firm. Tall, blond and handsome,'' Karyn said with an attempt at lightness.

''You must have a photo of him?''

''I don't need one,'' Karyn said. ''Fiona, I'm sorry. You mustn't take this personally—I don't talk about him to anyone.''

''I just hope he was good to you,'' Fiona said fiercely. ''My only standard of comparison is Rafe—I don't know what I'd do without him, I depend on him for so much.'' She sighed, tugging the ribbon from her braid and shaking out her long hair. ''It only takes one look from Rafe and my father settles right down. Money talks, I suppose.''

''Then I'm very glad you've got Rafe,'' Karyn said. She could have asked in just what capacity Fiona did have Rafe, for that, too, was a subject they'd never talked about. But didn't she already know the answer? "I think it's time for a shower."

"Me, too. What a drag—it takes forever to wash my hair." Fiona gave a wicked grin. "Maybe I'll cut it short, like yours."

"That'd get your mother's goat."

Karyn followed Fiona upstairs, going into her own room and staring out the window. Today Rafe had gone to London; she had no idea when he'd be back.

Restlessly she turned on the radio, wishing Fiona had never brought up the subject of Steve; even miles from home, memories of him had the power to disturb her. Then, as she looked around for the book she was reading, she realized she'd left it downstairs in the drawing room. Still dressed in her jodphurs, she headed for the back stairs.

Rafe was standing at the bottom of them. As her heart gave a great jolt in her chest, her socked foot slipped on the smooth wood. She stumbled, grabbed for the railing, missed it and fell forward, her knees banging against the next step. So fast she didn't have time to think, Rafe charged up the stairs and put his arms around her; her face was jammed into his chest. "Are you okay?" he demanded. "Did you hurt yourself? Karyn, answer me!"

Her own arms had gone around him in sheer reflex. Beneath her palms, through the thin cotton of his shirt, Karyn could feel the taut planes of his back, the hard curve of his spine. His heart was pounding under her cheek; his breath stirred her hair. Wasn't this closeness what she'd been desperate for? She wanted to stay here forever, she realized dazedly, and raised her head. "I—I'm fine. Silly of me to slip, I guess you startled me—I thought you were in London."

"I came back early..." His voice died away. His gaze

bored into hers as his hand rose to stroke a strand of hair from her cheek. His fingers weren't quite steady, each of them leaving a streak of fire on her skin. Unmasked, naked desire flared in his eyes, as vivid and dangerous as fire.

For the briefest of moments she yielded to that desire, her lashes drifting to her cheeks and her lips parting. Then, with a tiny sound of distress, Karyn shoved against Rafe's chest. Almost simultaneously, he pushed her away as hard as he could. Losing her balance, she gripped the banister, and from somewhere dredged up the shadow of a smile. "It won't help if we both fall down the stairs."

He was shaking his head like a man who'd just been struck a crippling blow. Or a man waking from a dream and finding himself in a harsh reality not of his choosing. "Hell's teeth," he muttered, "I swore that wasn't going to happen again."

He surged to his feet, pulling her with him, then holding her by the shoulders a careful distance from his body. "Are you sure you're all right?"

Her left knee hurt abominably. "This is unbearable—whatever it is that happens when I get within ten feet of you," she whispered. "Don't bother denying it, I know it happens to you, too."

"There's no point in denying it. I'm pulled to you every time I see you, I can't get you off my mind night or day—I wish to God we'd never met."

Because of Fiona, she thought wretchedly. Fiona, whom she already loved, and had unwittingly betrayed once again in that brief embrace on the stairs.

But wasn't there more, she thought with a sudden chill of her blood. Wasn't Rafe's charisma, his sheer sexuality, all too reminiscent of Steve? An icy hand clamped itself around her heart. Steve had swept her off her feet. Was she going to allow the exact same thing to happen again, this time with Rafe? ''You can't wish we'd never met any more strongly than I do,'' she said in a stony voice.

''Okay, so we've got that much straight,'' Rafe said harshly. ''We wish we hadn't met and we lust after each other. But we're not going to do one damn thing about it. If you hadn't fallen on the stairs, we—''

''So now it's my fault?''

''I didn't say that.''

''But you were thinking it.''

''For God's sake, Karyn, I don't know what's going on any more than you do! You think I like feeling this way every time I look at you? What's between you and me is an aberration. It'll pass. It's got to.''

''Who are you trying to convince, myself or you?''

Her cheeks were pink with temper and her lips, those delectable lips, were pressed firmly together. ''Both of us,'' he said with a wintry smile.

She said flatly, putting her suspicions into words, ''There isn't any chemistry between you and Fiona. Not one spark.''

''You let me worry about that,'' he grated, dropping his hands to his sides as though contact with her was poisonous. ''Where's Fiona?''

''In the shower. She uses enough water for ten people, that's one thing I've learned about her.'' Recklessly Karyn pressed her point. ''When you hug each other, it's almost as though you're brother and sister.''

''We're the best of friends,'' he snapped. ''Have you got a problem with that?''

How could she know? She'd assumed Steve was her friend as well as her lover, and had learned otherwise all too soon and with devastating consequences. Karyn bit her lip. ''But if there isn't any passion—''

''Passion's overrated. I went that way once, and she

ripped the heart from my body. So I swore off it. As for Fiona, she's too innocent to know the difference.''

Karyn said raggedly, ''What you feel for me—is that passion?''

His jaw tightened; he looked like a man being tormented. ''There's no point in even talking about it.''

He was right. But when he was standing so close to her that she could feel herself sinking into the dark blue of his irises, desire made nonsense of reason. Aching to touch him, longing to lift her lips to his and taste him, she burst out, ''How can you be Fiona's lover if there isn't any passion between you? I just don't understand how you can do that.''

''Her lover?'' he repeated blankly. ''What the hell do you mean?''

Karyn's temper flared. ''The usual. Two people who make love. In bed. What did you think I meant?''

''Fiona and I have never gone to bed together.''

''Rafe, I saw her going to your room one night.''

''Fiona hasn't been anywhere near my bedroom.''

''Don't lie to me! The way you kissed me that night under the trees, thinking I was Fiona—''

Clipping off each word, Rafe repeated, ''I am not and never have been Fiona's lover.''

Karyn gaped at him. ''Then why are you going to marry her?''

''Who says I'm going to?''

''Douglas.''

Rafe swore under his breath. ''He told you that?''

''The day he came to see me at the inn, he said an announcement was imminent.''

''Have you said anything to Fiona?''

''No!''

''Thank God for that.''

''Oh, let's keep Fiona in the dark,'' Karyn flared. ''After all, we're only talking about her life and her happiness.''

Rafe said tautly, ''Douglas wants Holden blue blood and Holden money in the family, and isn't above using a little leverage to get them. But he picked the wrong man to push around.''

''So are you going to marry Fiona?'' Karyn persisted, her chest tight.

Rafe jammed his hands in his pockets. ''I told Douglas I'd think about it.''

''If you have to think about it, you're sure not in any danger of succumbing to passion.''

''Since when did you become the expert?''

She flinched. Hadn't her marriage proved she wasn't even remotely an expert? ''I asked you a straightforward question about marrying Fiona,'' she retorted. ''Yes or no—either answer will do.''

''How about minding your own business?''

She had no part in his life. That's what he was saying. Torn between fury and an agony that would overwhelm her were she to let it in, Karyn muttered, ''I'll be delighted to stay out of your business. But don't you dare hurt Fiona!''

''I have no wish in the world to hurt Fiona.''

What more was there to say? Striving for normality, Karyn asked, ''Were you coming upstairs to look for one of us?''

''You, as it happens...I came to tell you that Clarissa and Douglas are giving a formal dinner party next week to welcome you into the family.''

Karyn's jaw dropped. ''They are?''

''Don't ask how I did it,'' Rafe said, his smile almost genuine. ''Just turn up.''

To spend the evening watching Rafe and Fiona side by side? With Douglas and Clarissa eying her every move?

Karyn said tersely, ''If you think I'm going to Willowbend after the way Douglas treated me, you're crazy.''

''It's an olive branch, Karyn. Take it and be glad. Besides, you'll get to meet my parents.''

Her eyes narrowed. ''I don't like other people controlling my life. Back off, Rafe.''

''You'll need an evening gown. You and Fiona could go shopping together.''

''You don't get it, do you? I have a life at home, a job I have to get back to—I can't wait around until next week.''

''Extend your holidays. Three or four days won't make any difference.''

''I don't own the clinic,'' she said nastily, ''I just work there.''

''Then I'll—''

He broke off as Fiona's bedroom door opened and Fiona called out, ''Karyn? Shall we raid the kitchen for tea and biscuits?''

''I haven't had a shower yet,'' Karyn called back, ''so give me ten minutes.'' Then she turned back to Rafe, lowering her voice. ''Don't you dare tell Fiona about the dinner—because it's not going to happen.''

She hurried back up to her bedroom, giving Fiona a distracted smile. ''Rafe's back, why don't you go and say hello to him?''

Then she went into the bathroom and turned on the water full blast. Hot water. She was under no illusions that cold water would be of any use whatsoever.

Fiona and Rafe had gone outside to sit on the patio under Karyn's window, where Fiona was trying to untangle her wet hair. ''I've had such a wonderful time with Karyn, Rafe. I'm really getting to know her—I can't thank you enough for bringing us together.''

Fiona made a beautiful picture as she combed out her hair in the last rays of the setting sun, a picture that left Rafe totally unmoved. Then she flipped her hair back so she could see him. "Well, except for one thing. Any mention of her husband and she spooks like a frightened pony."

"It's only a year since she was widowed."

"I think the hurt went so deep she can't talk about him."

But not so deep that she couldn't kiss me, Rafe thought savagely. The thought of Karyn in another man's arms, sharing another man's bed, nearly drove him out of his mind: not an insight he could share with anyone, especially not Fiona. "Perhaps she will when she's spent more time with you."

"Perhaps," Fiona said uncertainly. "Anyway, while she's in the shower, why don't we rummage in the kitchen for some of those chocolate-almond cookies, she loves them."

So when Karyn wiped the steam from the bathroom window, she saw Fiona and Rafe walking side by side across the garden. Knowing exactly what she was going to do, she wrapped herself in a towel and picked up the phone in her bedroom.

The secretary at the clinic answered, sounding as though she was across the room rather than across the ocean. Quickly Karyn asked for her boss. When he picked up the receiver, she said, "Dennis, it's Karyn. I was thinking I might come home a few days early, how would that fit in the schedule?"

"No kidding? Karyn, it'd be a godsend. Jim and Rita are both down with flu and the rest of us are trying to cover. Come as soon as you can, it'd be fine with me. Did you find your sister?"

Karyn gave him an edited version of events, rang off, called the airline and was lucky enough to get a cancellation for the very next evening. She booked a seat on the train, threw on some clothes and went downstairs to find Fiona and Rafe in the drawing room, with its gleaming cherrywood furniture and single vibrant Picasso. Fiona held out a plate of almond cookies coated in rich Belgian chocolate. "These are for you," she said. "Though if you felt like sharing them, I'm sure I could choke down a couple."

Feeling absurdly guilty, Karyn took one. "I'll have to take some of these home with me," she said lightly. "I called the clinic and they've had a flu outbreak. So I changed my flight and I'm going home tomorrow."

Fury flashed across Rafe's face, and then was gone as if it had never been. Fiona said in genuine dismay, "Tomorrow? Oh, Karyn, you can't go that soon."

"You can visit me, Fiona. Anytime."

"I could, couldn't I? But promise you'll come for Christmas. I'm sure by then Mother and Dad will be happy to see you."

Karyn wouldn't count on it. "That'd be lovely," she said.

"Mother always decorates with holly and hundreds of candles, it's so beautiful. And Rafe throws a huge party here at Stoneriggs on New Year's Eve, you'll have to come to that."

Maybe she'd break a leg the week before Christmas, Karyn thought wildly. Fall off a horse. Be trampled by a sick cow. "I don't have any fancy clothes."

"If you weren't going home tomorrow, we could go shopping in London," Fiona wailed. "It's much too soon for you to leave."

"I have to go. My boss has always been very good to me, and the least I can do is help out when they need me."

"In that case," Fiona said, "you and I are going to stay

up all night and talk. I don't want to waste a single minute.''

''I'm flying to Oslo early tomorrow morning, and I've got some paperwork to clear up before I go,'' Rafe said brusquely. ''So I won't see you again, Karyn—have a safe trip.''

Feeling as though her heart was being torn from her body, for the next time she saw him he might well be married to Fiona, Karyn said stiffly, ''Thanks for everything.''

''For heaven's sake,'' Fiona said impatiently, ''give her a kiss, Rafe. She's my sister!''

Praying that her wince of dismay had been invisible, Karyn stood as stiff as a china doll as Rafe chastely put his lips to her cheek. She didn't dare meet his eyes; she'd be finished if she did.

Rafe kissed Fiona on the cheek as well, and headed for his study as though pursued by a pack of wolves. By tomorrow night Karyn would be boarding a plane that would carry her four thousand miles away. Home, where she belonged.

He didn't want passion. So the sooner she went home, the better.

Four thousand miles sounded just fine to him.

CHAPTER FIVE

KARYN had spent the last couple of hours in the company of a cow with bloat. While the cow was feeling better for the encounter, it could by no stretch be called a romantic way to spend an afternoon. So why was she thinking about Rafe as she took the turn from the farmer's muddy driveway onto the highway?

She thought about him entirely too often, especially at night. Which wasn't romantic, either. It was painful and disturbing and made her very unhappy.

Rafe had awoken her body from its long sleep; and now, unfortunately, it wouldn't go back to its state of dormancy. Nor—so she'd discovered—could she substitute anyone other than Rafe. For the first time since she was widowed, she'd gone out on a couple of dates, one with another vet and one with a city planner from Charlottetown. Both were nice men, who'd kissed her good-night with enthusiasm; and both had left her cold. Rafe was the man she wanted.

Rafe was the man she couldn't have. So was she simply craving the forbidden?

She and Fiona kept in constant contact by e-mail. Often Fiona's e-mails mentioned Rafe's name; always they served as a reminder of him. Phrases stuck in Karyn's mind...*Rafe invited me to a dance at the castle last night, I wore a very classy silver dress...Rafe's off to New Zealand to check out a new hotel... Rafe's so incredibly good at keeping Mother and Dad off my back.* Even, occasionally, *Rafe says hello.* Upon which Karyn would grit her teeth and type back, *Hi to Rafe.*

At no time did Fiona say anything about Rafe proposing to her. Did that mean he'd decided against marrying her? Or that he was still thinking about it?

With a big sigh Karyn brought her attention back to the present. May had merged into June. The fields were green with sprouting corn and drills of potatoes; the cows looked sleek and well-fed. Then, as she wound down a long hill, her foot hit the brake. She always tried to avoid this road, but today her mind had been more on Rafe than on the route she'd chosen. To her right was the split-level where the Harveys lived with their young son, Donny. A bicycle was lying on the lawn; a red SUV was parked in the driveway. Saving Donny Harvey from drowning had cost Steve his life…

Next door to the Harveys was the house she and Steve had shared, an attractive blue Cape Cod.

Behind both houses lay the sinuous curve of the river.

Her hands were clenched around the wheel so tightly her wrists hurt. Steve was going to walk out the door, she thought wildly, in his gray business suit and expensive trench coat, his eyes a cold, pale blue.

She braked hard, pulling over onto the shoulder of the road. Her forehead dropped to the wheel; she squeezed her eyes shut, trying to obliterate the surge of ugly memories. Steve's face contorted with rage. The cruel grip of his fingers. His voice hammering at her, his endless questions, his prying into every corner of her life.

Worst of all, the sensation that—no matter where she went—he was watching her.

Karyn could hear her own breathing harsh in her ears. She raised her head. No one was walking out of the door of the blue house, she thought dully. No one.

A wave of exhaustion washed over her. No wonder she'd

repressed the two years of her marriage; the alternative was too frightening.

As though a lightbulb had been turned on, she suddenly realized that it didn't matter whether Rafe got engaged to Fiona or not. Didn't matter at all. Even if he stayed as free as—as that crow flying across the road—she couldn't possibly get involved with him.

How had she described Steve to Fiona? *Tall, blond and handsome.* Wasn't Rafe tall, dark and handsome? Charismatic, like Steve. Sexy like Steve. Dangerous like Steve. Because Rafe, like Steve, made her lose her head and melt in his arms in all-too-easy surrender.

How stupid she'd been the past ten days not to have figured this out! Instead she'd moped around the house, allowing dreams and fantasies of Rafe to dominate her life.

No more, she decided militantly. She should have driven past Steve's house long before this; it had just taught her a salutary lesson.

She simply wasn't ready to get involved with anyone: city planner, veterinarian or one of the richest men in England. Maybe she never would be. There'd be no more dates, no more kisses on the front step; and no more mooning over a black-haired man she wouldn't kiss on the doorstep or anywhere else. In fact, if Rafe did get engaged it could be seen as a bonus, in case she backslid.

For the first time, she felt glad to be home.

It wasn't quite as easy as Karyn had anticipated to oust Rafe from her thoughts. She still dreamed about him regularly, waking with her body aching with unfulfilled desire. As well, his face would flash across her mind at the most inconvenient times; she'd want to share a joke with him, or tell him about the horse whose colic she'd cured. Instead she e-mailed Fiona with all the events of her day.

However, as time passed, Fiona's responses became less frequent, and stopped mentioning Rafe altogether. Stopped mentioning anything very much. With a perplexed frown, Karyn read a message from her sister that described the raspberry crop and the slugs in the lettuce in exhaustive detail. *I'm glad the raspberries are fine and the slugs aren't,* she e-mailed back, *but how are you?* For four days she didn't hear a word. Then, as she entered the house after work one afternoon, tired from a nine-hour shift, the phone was ringing. She wasn't on call. But she'd better get it anyway.

"Karyn? It's Fiona."

"Are you all right?" Karyn demanded. "I've been worried about you."

"Oh, Karyn, I can't tell you how happy I am! I've fallen in love. Head over heels in love."

With Rafe, Karyn thought with a sick jolt in her chest. And why not? The lack of chemistry between Fiona and Rafe, which Karyn had noticed and Rafe hadn't denied, was because Fiona hadn't been in love with her friend of so many years. But now she was.

"It happened so suddenly," Fiona burbled on, "between one moment and the next—just like in the books. Love at first sight… I don't care if it's a cliché, it's absolutely true and so wonderful I don't even know how to describe it."

She had to say something. Injecting as much warmth in her voice as she could, Karyn said, "Congratulations… although I'd hardly call it love at first sight."

"He's such a lovely man, why didn't I ever notice that before? Oh, Karyn, I suppose I shouldn't say this, but he kisses like a dream. Absolutely delicious…"

Karyn knew he did. Her heart congealing into a cold lump in her rib cage, she muttered, "Perhaps you were too close to him to really appreciate him before this."

"I don't know what you mean—I'd only seen him a couple of times."

Karyn frowned. "What are you talking about? You've known him all your life."

"All my life?" Fiona repeated in a puzzled voice. "No, I haven't. Although it feels like I've been waiting for him all my life." She gave a delighted giggle. "I'm going away with him this weekend and I'm not even nervous about it. He just feels so right, Karyn. So absolutely perfect."

Karyn said faintly, "Are you or are you not talking about Rafe?"

"*Rafe?* Goodness, no, whatever gave you that idea? I couldn't possibly fall in love with Rafe! I'm talking about John."

Karyn sat down hard on the floor, wondering if she was going out of her mind. She said evenly, "Fiona, will you please begin at the beginning? I thought you meant you'd fallen in love with Rafe."

"You must be joking," Fiona said blithely. "Rafe's like a brother to me. He's never been remotely like a lover."

Sounding like a robot, fully aware that Rafe had already given her this information, Karyn said, "You've never been Rafe's lover."

"Nope—not even close." Fiona sighed. "Mother and Dad would love me to get engaged to Rafe, they've been dropping very broad hints in that direction lately. They're not going to be too happy when they find out I'm passionately in love with someone else and want to marry him instead…but they should have known Rafe was never in the running."

"So tell me about John," Karyn mumbled, her emotions in a turmoil.

"John Settler. Fourth son of an earl, so that's all right. And he's got more than enough money for the two of us, although nothing like what Rafe has, of course. Because he's not content to live off his inheritance, he apprenticed as a cabinetmaker, and now he makes the most beautiful furniture that he sells at outrageous prices. I'd seen him around town once or twice, but we'd never connected. Then Mother invited him to the house to see if he could design a wardrobe for her bedroom, and that was that. Game over. We were head over heels in love."

How ironic that Clarissa herself had precipitated what must have been a bitter blow to her. "What does he look like?"

"Didn't I tell you? Brown hair and deep brown eyes and a beard, and he's the kindest man I've ever met." With a maturity new to her, Fiona added, "I think kindness can go a long way, don't you?"

Steve had been anything but kind. "I do, yes."

"He thinks I'm wonderful and he makes me laugh. Karyn, I'm so happy!" After a telltale hesitation, Fiona added shyly, "We've been to bed together—that was lovely, too. I'd never done it before. I'm glad John was the first."

"I—I didn't realize you'd never been to bed with anyone. We never talked about that."

"There've been men who've kissed me in a loverlike kind of way. Trying it on, I suppose. Even Rafe did that once, one evening at Willowbend." Fiona paused thoughtfully. "About the time you turned up."

Karyn would be willing to bet Rafe had kissed Fiona right after a very different kiss under the oak trees. As Fiona chattered on, she struggled to pay attention. Fiona finished by saying with a touching new confidence, "Even though I haven't told my parents yet, John and I will be getting married this summer. You'll be sure to come for the wedding and be my maid of honor? Floral colors in chiffon, I thought, and lots of sweet peas and garden flowers. Don't you think that sounds pretty?"

"Beautiful," Karyn said, and asked the critical question. "Will you invite Rafe?"

Sounding shocked, Fiona replied, "Of course I will. I couldn't get married without Rafe being there."

"Does he know about John?"

"Oh, yes. I tell Rafe everything. He was a bit taken aback at first, and who can blame him? So was I! But he's really happy for me." Again Fiona paused. "Almost relieved, in a way that I don't quite understand. Maybe he'd been worrying about my single state...by the way, did I tell you how sweet John is with the animals at the shelter?"

"You didn't, no." With heartfelt warmth Karyn said, "Fiona, your news took me by surprise, too. But I'm delighted for you...I wish you and John years of happiness together. And guess what—I get a new brother-in-law out of the deal."

"The best one in the whole world. Promise you'll come to the wedding?"

"All right," Karyn gulped, "I promise...let me know the date, won't you? I'll talk to you soon. Love you."

"You, too. 'Bye, Karyn."

Karyn scrambled to her feet, replaced the receiver and stared blankly at the wall.

Rafe was never going to marry Fiona, because Fiona had—in all innocence—fallen in love with someone else. She, Karyn, would never have to cope with Rafe as her sister's husband, or as the father of her sister's children.

For a moment sheer relief transfixed her. She felt as though a huge weight had been lifted from her shoulders, leaving her light and suffused with unthinking happiness; as though she could dance around the kitchen.

But in all too rapid succession, that thought was followed

by another. What she'd come to view as a safety net was no longer in place. Rafe was a free man. He'd even been relieved to hear Fiona was in love with someone else.

Why had he been relieved?

Why did it matter? After driving past Steve's house a couple of weeks ago, she'd decided Rafe's marital status was immaterial to her; because of the long shadow Steve had cast, she wasn't even ready to date anyone.

She'd believed her own assertions, wholeheartedly. For exactly fourteen days.

Now they were wavering like flags in the breeze.

Thank heavens Rafe lived four thousand miles away. All she had to do was pray that he stay there.

As the golden light of evening streamed through the window, it seemed obvious to Karyn that Rafe would stay safely in England, where he belonged. A man of enormous wealth, he'd just been supplanted by a cabinetmaker, the fourth son of an earl. No, Rafe wouldn't hightail it to a small island across the Atlantic in hot pursuit of Fiona's twin sister.

A ridiculous prospect. Besides, she shouldn't flatter herself she was that important to him.

But that night, when the stars were glimmering coldly through the skylight over her bed, Karyn wasn't so sanguine. She remembered with searing clarity every moment she'd spent with Rafe, from the spark that had leaped between them on that first encounter in the woods, to the heat of his body when he'd shielded her on the stairs at Stoneriggs.

None of this had been trivial. She couldn't pretend that it had been: to minimize his feelings or hers would be an insult to both of them. She burrowed into the pillow, wishing with all her heart that she'd never met him.

If she hadn't, she'd never have met Fiona; who'd enriched her life so immeasurably.

When Karyn did finally fall asleep, she didn't dream about Rafe, as she'd expected to. She dreamed about Steve. It was the same dream that had haunted her ever since his death; a dream saturated with a terror all the more powerful for being amorphous. It was only at the end of the dream, after she'd been running through endless dark alleyways, her breath sobbing in her ears, that she burst out into the open and saw, right in front of her, her husband, Steve. He had a gun in his hand, and was slowly lifting it to point at her heart.

She always woke up just as his finger tightened on the trigger. Tonight was no exception. Her pulses racing, her body rigid, Karyn stared up at the night sky and knew she had her answer. It didn't matter what Rafe did, whether he got engaged to ten different women or moved to Antarctica. He wasn't for her.

Everything that could go wrong the next day did. An elderly dog Karyn had been medicating against kidney failure succumbed to the disease, leaving her with the unenviable task of breaking the bad news to the dog's equally elderly owner. One of the other vets called in sick, doubling her workload in the clinic. This was followed, four hectic hours later, by an emergency call. A farmer's flock of sheep was threatened with an outbreak of orf, a disease as nasty as it sounded; she and another vet labored long and hard for the rest of the day in the open fields to vaccinate the whole flock. It was backbreaking work, which left her covered in mud and physically exhausted. But at least her shift was finished. Over two and a half hours ago, she thought wryly as she drove home, an old tarp between her trousers and the car seat.

A hot bath and a Greek pizza with extra feta and black olives. That'd fix her up.

She turned the last corner and drove down her street; her mother's house, which she'd inherited, was at the very end of the road, enclosed in a small grove of birches. The Camdens' garden halfway down the street was in full bloom; one of Karyn's plans, when things slowed down at work, was to tackle the garden. Peonies, maybe, and lots of Shasta daisies. Fiona liked peonies.

A car was parked in her driveway. She slewed to a stop.

It looked just like Steve's car.

A whimper of fear burst from her lips. Wasn't that what the dream was about? And wasn't that, irrationally, still her living nightmare? That, somehow, Steve hadn't really died. Instead he'd been lying in wait for the last year, playing with her, cat and mouse. Wanting her to build a false sense of security before he knocked it to the ground and engulfed her once again.

There was a man standing in the shadow of the lace vine that had entwined the front porch. As he sighted her, he walked down the steps toward her.

A man with black hair. Not blond. It wasn't Steve. It was Rafe.

Very slowly Karyn climbed out of her car.

Rafe took one look at her face and grabbed her by the arm. ''Karyn! For God's sake, what's wrong?''

His voice, the breeze flattening his shirt to his chest, the concern in his face: had she ever forgotten anything about him? ''I—I thought you were someone—I mean, it startled me, seeing you there.''

His eyes narrowed. ''Who did you think I was?''

She tugged her arm free and took refuge in anger. ''Nobody! What are you doing here, Rafe Holden? I don't recall inviting you for a visit.''

He suddenly grinned at her, a boyish grin so full of charm and so laden with male energy that she took an instinctive step back. "You didn't. I figured if I asked, you'd say no. So I came anyway. Just like you with the Talbots. That worked, didn't it?"

"You're so right—I would have said no."

"I'm taking you out for dinner." He looked her up and down, from the toes of her mud-caked, steel-toed boots to the streak of dirt on her cheek. "Not many restaurants would let you in the door right now."

"Some of us work for our living."

His grin widened. "You can't insult me that easily, Karyn."

"I'll work on it."

"You do that." Before she could duck, he reached out and ruffled her hair. "It's great to see you."

It was a huge effort not to smile back. "I wish I could say the same. You realize you've turned up one day after Fiona told me she's going to marry John."

"No sense in wasting time."

"Are you looking for sympathy?"

"I'd already decided I couldn't possibly marry Fiona."

"I'm supposed to believe that?"

"I'd prefer you did…it happened the first time I saw Fiona and John together. They looked so gloriously happy, so wrapped up in each other." He hesitated. "I figured if Fiona could break every one of her parents' rules, I could damn well drop in to see you. So here I am." He looked her up and down, laughter lurking in his dark blue eyes. "Did you spend your day mud-wrestling?"

With an exasperated sigh, Karyn straightened her aching back. "I vaccinated thirty-three sheep, not one of whom wanted to be anywhere near me or the syringe. You should try it sometime. It's a humbling experience."

He laughed outright. "Looks as though they won."

"There was one ewe who nearly did." She wouldn't smile. She wouldn't. "I'm going inside, having a hot bath and ordering a pizza. You can drive right back to the airport and fly home."

"That's not very hospitable of you."

Now she did smile. "You can't insult me that easily, Rafe."

"I can't fly home. I have pictures of Fiona and John. She'd never speak to me again if I didn't show them to you."

"Pass them over. Then vamoose."

"Not a hope," he said. "We're going out for dinner, I have it all planned." He glanced over his shoulder. "This was your mother's house, wasn't it?"

"My neighbor, Bob Camden, used to be a fullback. If I tell him you're bothering me, he'll turn you inside out."

"I scarcely think so. Have you heard of a black belt in karate? Oh Karyn, you look so cute when you're angry."

"Don't patronize me!"

"You also look worn-out." He took her by the arm and steered her toward the house. "Where are your keys?"

His fingers burned through her shirtsleeve, and briefly her mind went blank. How could she think when all she really wanted to do was fling her arms around him and kiss him until she couldn't breathe?

She fumbled in her backpack for the house key and inserted it in the front door with a clumsiness that horrified her. In a wash of the same terror that had overwhelmed her the night before, she looked up at him and said with raw truth, "Rafe, you scare the life out of me. I can't afford to be hurt again, I just can't!"

So she was still grieving her husband, Rafe thought; vehemently he wished it were otherwise. ''The last thing I want to do is hurt you.''

''Then go home and leave me alone.''

''No. Not yet,'' he said, a note in his voice she'd never heard before, and that terrified her with its implacability.

''What are you doing here anyway?'' she cried.

''Waiting for you to get ready so we can eat. It's four hours later for me—I'm hungry.''

She let out her breath in a hiss of fury. ''There are lots of restaurants in Charlottetown that'd be delighted to feed you. Then you can get the first flight to Halifax and catch the red-eye to England—you've got plenty of time.''

''I traveled in my own jet,'' Rafe said calmly, ''it's at the Charlottetown airport. While you're unlacing those godawful boots, I'll start a bath for you.''

''Pardon me, of course you'd have your own jet,'' she snarled. ''And they're very practical boots—you try being stepped on by a 1,700-pound bull.''

She dumped her pack on the porch floor. It was just as well Rafe didn't know that underneath her green man-tailored shirt and her taupe canvas pants—work clothes that served her well when she had to wrestle sheep—she was wearing an ivory silk bra lavishly decorated with lace. Sexy underwear was her one indulgence—that, and her scent. She'd always loved frivolous underclothes. But Steve hadn't approved of them; in one of his vicious flares of rage, he'd accused her of being on the make when she went to work at the clinic with lace hidden under her work clothes.

As if she'd had the time or the inclination to look for another man. But to keep the peace she'd put away all her pretty underwear, wearing cotton jockey shorts and grey cotton bras instead.

''You're a long way away,'' Rafe said.

Her lashes flickered. ''Oh. Yes. Sorry.''

''What were you thinking about?''

''I'm tired, that's all,'' she said shortly, and bent to undo her laces.

Light as gossamer, Rafe's lips slid across her nape. Before she could react, he walked away from her, crossing the hall and starting up the stairs. Of its own accord her hand reached up to cup the back of her neck and her eyes closed. Nothing had changed. She still wanted him.

Although *wanted* didn't seem in any way to express the tumult of longing and desire that had flooded her at that briefest of caresses. She could add panic to the mix, she thought helplessly. The man scared her out of her wits.

Steve had scared her out of her wits. Oh God, what was going on?

After unlacing her second boot, she lined it up on the mat with the first one. She could hear footsteps overhead, then the sound of water filling the tub, ordinary domestic sounds that reignited her fury. Okay, so Rafe had taken her by surprise, and she'd thought he was Steve. But she'd had time to recover and be damned if he was going to have it all his own way.

She marched up the stairs. The bathroom was engulfed in steam and the glorious fragrance of freesias. She read the label on the bottle standing on the vanity, and said blankly, ''Where did that come from?''

''I brought it with me.''

''That stuff costs the earth.''

''Hardly.''

''You can't go giving me expensive presents!''

''Wear something casual,'' he said. ''You'll like where we're going.''

In a low voice Karyn said, ''Rafe, don't ride over me

like that. As though I don't exist.'' Wasn't that what Steve had done, time and time again?

Rafe stood still, gazing at her. She looked exhausted, he thought with compunction. When she'd first seen him this evening, she'd been terrified; he'd swear to that in a court of law. So was he in danger of hurting her just by being here? Leaning over to turn off the taps before he had a flood on his hands, he said, ''I have more money than I know what to do with, and that's a very small gift. All I want is to give you pleasure, Karyn—and don't ever think you don't exist for me.''

She didn't know what frightened her more, his gentleness or his willpower. ''Where were you planning to eat?''

''Will you trust me enough to put yourself in my hands?''

''That's one heck of a big question,'' she said with a flash of defiance.

''I only meant as far as dinner's concerned,'' Rafe said with very little regard for the truth; and to his relief saw her slow nod of agreement. If only he knew more about Karyn's husband; then maybe he wouldn't have the sensation that with every move he made, he was stepping into a minefield.

Surely her husband wasn't anything to do with the white-faced terror with which she'd greeted him?

Now that he was here, he was going to make it his business to find out about Steven Patterson. While he could have set his investigator on Steve a long time ago, something in Rafe had shrunk from such a course. Yes, he'd needed to investigate Karyn, for Fiona's sake as well as his own. But he wanted Karyn herself to tell him about Steve. ''I'll wait for you downstairs,'' Rafe said, and suited action to word.

He didn't want to be waiting downstairs, Rafe thought

as he wandered through the pleasant, unpretentious living room to the small dining alcove that overlooked the birch trees and a field of new corn. He wanted to be in Karyn's bed. But all those years ago when he'd been learning to ride cross-country, hadn't he been warned never to rush his fences? It was advice he should take to heart right now.

He glanced around at the eclectic collection of books and magazines, at the brightly colored cushions and the few carefully chosen ornaments. On the stereo-stand there was a photo of a smiling couple in their forties: Karyn's adoptive parents, he'd be willing to bet. But although he prowled through the whole downstairs, he didn't find a single photo of the man who'd been Karyn's husband.

One more piece of evidence that Karyn was so deeply sunk in grief she couldn't bear to be reminded of Steve.

Feeling restless and unsettled, Rafe went outdoors to wait for her.

CHAPTER SIX

KARYN came downstairs ten minutes later. Her hair was an aureole of soft curls around her face; her brief blue denim skirt was topped by a figure-hugging sweater in soft pink mohair. Her legs were bare, her feet in flat, thin-strapped sandals. For a moment that was outside of time Rafe stared at her. For six years he'd had his defences firmly in place. He'd dated, had brief affairs and had never allowed anyone to tap the deep well of passion that Celine had desecrated. Everything easy, and according to his own rules.

The woman standing in front of him could breach those defences all too quickly. Or had she already done so?

Karyn said uncomfortably, "Am I too dressed up?"

Rafe pulled himself together. "You look beautiful," he said. "Isn't that the wool you bought in Hart's Run?"

"I unraveled the sweater the first time, it would have fit me if I'd been pregnant with triplets. The second time it came out a bit small, but I couldn't be bothered to try again."

"I like it just as it is," he said, and managed to keep his gaze above the level of her breasts.

She blushed, lowered her eyes and muttered, "I just wish I knew why—"

"Dinner first," he said. "We'll talk later. I want to go in the general direction of Stanhope."

As she got in his rented car, she thought out various routes, instantly discarding the one that went past the house she and Steve had lived in. "I'll navigate," she said. "Have you made a reservation in Stanhope?"

''You'll see.'' He got in the driver's seat and took an envelope out of the dash. ''Fiona sent this. With her love.''

The envelope was tied with pink ribbon, smelled faintly of lilies of the valley and contained several photos. In each one, Fiona looked radiant, her arm linked with a pleasant-faced, bearded man not much taller than she, who also looked extremely happy. Karyn spoke without thinking. ''I've never seen Fiona look like that…he must be quite a guy.'' Then she added awkwardly, ''I didn't mean that you—''

''Thinking I could marry Fiona was a classic case of self-deception,'' Rafe said dryly. ''You were the one who said there wasn't any chemistry between us, and you were right. Luckily Fiona met John. You can imagine Clarissa and Douglas's reaction—but Fiona stood her ground as though she'd been defying her parents since the day she was born.''

''She said you helped.''

''I pointed out a few basic facts to Douglas—but Fiona took him on first. All by herself.''

''Good for her,'' Karyn said. ''Anyone who can make an impression on Douglas Talbot has my undying admiration. Which doesn't include you,'' she added. ''All you had to do was wave your money in front of him—that doesn't count.''

''Pity,'' Rafe said, his smile crackling with energy. ''I'd like to have your undying admiration.''

''For someone who'll never have it, you look entirely too pleased with yourself.''

For someone who didn't know what the hell he was doing, he felt entirely too pleased with himself. And with her. Deciding to keep that piece of information to himself, Rafe said, ''I love Fiona. I've known her since she was a babe in arms, I taught her how to climb trees and jump her first pony over a stone wall, and I'm delighted she's found someone she adores. John's a fine fellow—they're admirably suited.''

''I wired her a huge bouquet of flowers,'' Karyn said. ''I do so want her to be happy.''

''She will be, I'm sure. What's the name of this river?''

Karyn started describing the countryside. Rafe's questions were penetrating and his interest unfeigned; she expanded, forgetting how angry she was with him, allowing her intelligence full rein, and hearing herself being wittier than usual. Before she knew it, they'd reached the north shore with its miles of sand beaches and red cliffs. Instead of turning toward the restaurants in the area, Rafe parked alongside the beach. Karyn got out, watching as he took a large wicker hamper from the trunk. ''Picnic,'' he said economically. ''Let's find a table where we can see the water.''

''A picnic?''

''Is that okay?''

''It's a wonderful idea—I love picnics!''

She looked as entranced as a little girl on Christmas morning. Rafe turned away, wanting to kiss her so badly his whole body was on fire with need. He slammed the trunk shut and walked along the boardwalk. Some picnic tables had been set on a grass verge overlooking the long stretch of surf; he dumped the hamper on the furthest one. ''Let's eat.''

Karyn unlatched the lid and peered inside, lifting out one of the delicate china plates with its hand-painted pattern of flowering herbs. ''It's a work of art,'' she marveled. ''Don't tell me those are lobster rolls—my favorite.''

''There's caviar and chicken, as well, and an avocado salad. Not to mention dessert.''

''Chocolate?'' she said hopefully.

"Dark chocolate mousse with truffles and hazelnuts."

Karyn laughed out loud. "I've died and gone to heaven."

He took out two crystal champagne flutes and the bottle of champagne that had been wrapped in a towel to keep it chilled. "We'll start with this."

She raised her brows. "A high-class picnic."

"Not quite the best money can buy," he grinned, "but getting close."

The cork came out with a most satisfying pop, bubbles rising like foam on the shore. Rafe raised his glass and for a moment was tongue-tied. He knew what he wanted to say. At least he thought he did. But it was way too soon. He drawled, "May all the vaccinated sheep be as healthy as horses."

"I'll drink to that." Then she unwrapped a crusty roll crammed with lobster, crisp celery and a deliciously tangy dressing and began to eat.

Rafe dug into the caviar, enjoying her pleasure in what was, by his standards, a very simple meal. The wind from the ocean was playing with her curls; her eyes were a deeper blue than the sea, although just as full of mysterious depths. Color tinted her cheeks. Helping her to salad, Rafe began to talk about his newest hotel, located on New Zealand's South Island.

Eventually Karyn had eaten her fill. She licked the last smear of chocolate from her spoon. "That was incredible. If I ate like this every day, I'd be as fat as a barrel."

"You're too thin."

"You're supposed to say I'm perfect," she responded pertly. "This was a much better choice than a restaurant, Rafe, thank you so much. I feel like a new woman."

"You've got chocolate on your chin," he said, leaned forward and wiped it off with one finger.

His face was so close she could have counted his eyelashes. If she'd been able to count. "Rafe, why are you here?" she blurted.

He poured two demitasses of coffee from a thermos, taking his time. "To bring you Fiona's photos—much as she loves you, she can't tear herself away from John right now to give them to you herself."

"There's a marvelous invention called the post office. What's the real reason?"

He had no intention of giving his cards away too soon; he'd learned a thing or two about strategy over the years. "I'm checking out a possible hotel purchase in Toronto and thought I'd drop in on the way."

She gave a rude snort. "Toronto's 2,500 miles away. You can skip that one, too."

"It's for real," he said mildly. "I travel hundreds of thousands of miles a year, a detour like this is nothing. Besides, you're Fiona's sister, and I wanted to see how you were."

"So it's nothing to do with that kiss in the woods?"

"Only if we want it to be."

Karyn said with a careful lack of emphasis, "I like my life the way it is. Sure, we lust after each other—so what? We aren't going to do anything about it."

"You're right, we aren't," he said cheerfully. "So you won't mind if I hang around for a day or two."

"It's a free country—I can't stop you," she said coldly.

"We'll go for dinner somewhere fancy tomorrow. What time do you have to be at work the next day?"

"I'm on the late shift," she said, eying him suspiciously.

"Good. Pack a toothbrush."

"I'm not going anywhere overnight with—"

"I've never in my life taken anything from a woman that

she wasn't willing to give, and I don't plan to start with you.''

His jaw was a tense line, his eyes unsmiling. Karyn said slowly, ''I hurt your feelings.''

''Yeah, you did.''

She could have apologized. But hadn't she spent a great deal of time apologizing to Steve, often for things that weren't her fault? She said coolly, ''You're a big boy, Rafe, you can handle it. Where are we going for dinner?''

''It'll be a surprise. I guarantee you'll like it and that you'll have a good time—how's that for arrogance?''

''You took the word out of my mouth.''

He gave a snort of laughter. ''Wear your best dress. There's live music, too—do you like to dance?''

''Dance with you—no way!''

''Why not?'' he asked blandly.

''I'd jump on you on the dance floor,'' she said, her scowl deepening.

''Fine by me.''

''You've got a one-track mind.''

He said deliberately, ''Did you ever feel that way about Steve?''

She surged to her feet in a move from which all her natural grace had been stripped. ''I don't want to talk about Steve!''

''Then we won't,'' Rafe said, all his senses on high alert. ''Tell me about the clinic instead. Or the teacher you had a crush on in grade seven.''

Karyn was wringing her hands; he was almost sure she didn't know she was doing it. ''I have to be at work at eight tomorrow morning,'' she said, ''we should go back.''

''A ten-minute walk on the beach first. It's a glorious sunset.''

He was putting the food and plates back in the basket.

Feeling trapped and beleaguered, Karyn said choppily, ''I'm not playing hard to get. I'm not interested in your money and I couldn't care less about your status.''

Rafe knew the truth when he heard it. ''Good,'' he said. ''With regards to my money, you're in a minority of two—you and Fiona...I'll put the hamper back in the car and meet you on the beach.''

So Karyn wandered down to the sand by herself, slipping off her sandals and letting the smooth grains slide between her toes. The surf's endless rhythms laved her ears; a pair of terns swooped in elegant curves over the white crests. I can handle Rafe, she thought in a surge of confidence, and walked down to the water's edge, letting the marbled foam wash over her feet. It was numbingly, bone-achingly cold.

With a tiny shriek she leaped backward. Into Rafe's arms.

She stood very still, watching the mosaic of orange and gold light dance on the sea as the sun's brilliant disc was slowly swallowed by the horizon. His hands were clasping her shoulders; he'd pulled her into his body, her back to his chest, his cheek to her ear. The heavy thud of his heart, the strength of his fingers, the waft of his breath in her hair, each was an astonishing intimacy, somehow bound up with the elemental powers of the ocean. Karyn closed her eyes, savoring every sensation, until her body was suffused with a liquid heat. Only then did she turn to face him.

The strong planes of his face were lit by the dying rays of the sun; his eyes, eyes that held the darkness of night, were fastened on her. She knew what was going to happen and welcomed it, opening to him before his lips as much as touched hers.

Rafe slid his arms around her, his hands stroking the soft wool of her sweater; he felt like a teenager before his first kiss, he thought dimly. He also felt as though he held the whole world in his arms.

She was a woman. Just a woman.

Then his mouth found the soft, delicious curve of her lips, and in an upwelling of pure sensation he stopped thinking altogether. Plunging with his tongue, savoring the fluid sweetness that was Karyn, he pulled her tight to him, molding her to his body. His groin had hardened instantly. Rather than pulling away, she pressed herself into him, trembling very lightly, her fingernails digging into his back.

He slid his mouth down the taut line of her throat, nuzzling the pulse in the hollow at its base where her blood was racing in tandem with his. Pushing her sweater aside, he found the silken curve of her shoulder, tasting, licking, nibbling until he wondered if he'd go out of his mind. The rise of her breast fit his palm perfectly; her nipple was as hard as a tiny shell. She moaned his name, cupped his face in her hands and pulled his mouth down to hers.

When he opened his eyes, hers, blazingly blue, were so close he could drown in them. Was drowning in them, he thought, and somehow found his voice. "Karyn, someone's coming—we've got an audience."

Another couple, hand in hand, was wandering toward them down the beach. She said dazedly, "Do we care?"

He wanted to protect her, he realized. From everything, including prying eyes. "I care," he said. "What's between us is private."

Karyn stepped back. The sand underfoot was both wet and cold, bringing her to her senses. "The only thing between us is old-fashioned lust," she said faintly.

"Even if that's true, it's still our concern. Not anyone else's."

He turned her to face the sea again, his arms wrapped around her body, hands linked at her waist. She leaned back, glad of his support because her knees felt as wobbly as jellyfish. She herself felt desired, sensual and fully alive, sheltered in the heat of Rafe's body. Had she ever luxuriated so instinctively in the pleasure of being held?

The sun had disappeared; the distant clouds were painted all the shades of pink and gold. She murmured, "I love the sea, don't you?"

"I own a little place in the Outer Hebrides, you can hear the surf through every window."

The other couple had passed them. Even though he yearned to continue a kiss that had stunned him with its potency, Rafe said easily, "I should get you home."

Karyn sighed, reluctant to leave even though she knew he was right. A romantic sunset, a beautiful beach, a man whose body entranced her: they'd all worked their spell. But now the spell was broken, and home was where she belonged. Back to reality, she thought ruefully, loosing the clasp of his hands and stepping away from him. "The water was like ice," she remarked, trying to mask how suddenly and inexplicably bereft she felt.

"Have you ever swum in the Bahamas? Or the Mediterranean?"

Steve had taken her to St. Lucia once; it had been a disaster from beginning to end, his obsessive jealousy poisoning every breath she took. She said evasively, "It must be lovely."

You're going to experience it very soon, thought Rafe. With me. What had started here, on an island beach, could only be continued. He took her by the hand and side by side they walked back to the car.

There were four vehicles left in the lot. A family was just getting into a red SUV, parents and a little boy.

Karyn's eyes widened in horror. She tried to duck behind

Rafe, but she was too late. The boy was waving at her. "Hey, Mum," he yelled, "there's Karyn!"

The woman's head swiveled around. "Karyn," she called, and after the smallest of hesitations walked over to them, followed by her husband and the little boy. "How nice to see you. Wasn't the sunset beautiful?"

Passionately wishing they'd met anyone else at the beach but this particular family, Karyn quickly made the introductions. "Sheila and Duncan Harvey, and their son, Donny. This is Rafe Holden, who's visiting from England."

If Duncan recognized the name, he was discreet enough not to mention it. He made some commonplace remark to Rafe as Donny ran over to Karyn, grabbing her by the skirt. She ruffled his tangled red curls; he smelled of salt water and seaweed. They all chatted for a few minutes, then Duncan said heartily, "We'd better get this fella back home, it's past his bedtime. Nice to have met you, Rafe. Karyn, we'll see you around."

Sheila gave Karyn a brief, hard hug. Then Karyn got into Rafe's car as fast as she could and busied herself fastening her seat belt. Rafe got in, too. His intuition operating in high gear, he said casually, "The little guy, Donny—he's got a crush on you?"

She bit her lip. "You could say so."

He put his hand on her wrist. "What's up, Karyn? There was something off-key about all that."

Dark hair feathered his forearm; she felt that inner shiver he could arouse in her simply by existing. If he'd had her investigated, he could do the same for Steve; she wouldn't put it past him. She said tonelessly, "My husband, Steve, saved Donny's life when the boy fell through the ice on the river near their house. Steve saw what was happening through the window—we were neighbors of the Harveys.

But after he'd lifted Donny onto the thicker ice, the current got hold of Steve and pulled him under the ice. They found his body two days later.''

Whatever Rafe had expected, it hadn't been this. ''I'm so sorry,'' he said. ''No wonder Sheila hugged you—and no wonder it's difficult to see them. They must feel so incredibly grateful, yet horribly guilty at the same time. I understand perfectly why you sold the house you and Steve were living in.''

Karyn made an indeterminate noise. She was sure it hadn't occurred to Steve that he might drown should he try and rescue a small boy from the river; Steve had never believed in his own mortality. However, the fact that he'd died in the act of saving a little boy's life still filled her with complex and conflicting emotions. She'd been freed from the terrible prison her marriage had become, no question of that; yet his last action couldn't help but redeem him in her eyes. It also made her feel unutterably sad.

How could she possibly explain all this to Rafe? She scarcely understood it herself.

Karyn was very quiet all the way back; and Rafe was busy with his own thoughts. So Steve had been a hero, who'd lost his life saving a small boy from drowning. How could Rafe possibly fault that? Yet he was jealous of a dead man.

Despicable, he thought. What kind of lowlife are you?

Doing his best to concentrate on the road, Rafe found himself for the second time wondering whether Karyn had directed him to take an unnecessary detour near Heddingley; he had an excellent sense of direction. He said nothing. After he'd parked in her driveway, he got out of the car and lifted the hamper from the trunk. ''Have the leftovers for lunch tomorrow, Karyn.''

She took the hamper from him, holding it like a shield in front of her. ''Good night,'' she said awkwardly.

''I'll pick you up tomorrow at six, does that give you enough time?''

She should say no. End this now. Everything rational within her told her to do just that. ''Plenty of time,'' she said, turned on her heel and hurried into the house.

Rafe waited until she was indoors before driving back to his hotel in the city. He hadn't actually lied this evening about his reasons for seeking Karyn out; just prevaricated. His father, Reginald, was a demon bridge player who early on had taught Rafe one rule: play your cards close to your chest. It was a rule that had often stood Rafe in good stead.

With Karyn, was he playing the game of his life, with passion as the wild card? Would he win or lose?

Did his happiness depend on the answer?

As soon as she got in the house, Karyn phoned her best friend, Liz Gaudet, who managed to combine being a wife, a nurse and a mother without losing either her sanity or her warmth. ''Liz? This is an emergency. I've been invited for dinner somewhere really fancy tomorrow night. What will I wear?''

''Wow. Where? Who with?''

Karyn swallowed. ''I don't know where. I'll be with Rafe Holden—I told you about him. My sister Fiona's friend.''

''The filthy rich Rafe Holden?''

''Who's used to sophisticated jet-setters in designer labels and makeup by Elizabeth Arden.''

''He hasn't asked them out for dinner. He's asked you. Okay, let's think.''

''I had lots of evening clothes when I was married because Steve and I used to go to insurance bashes. But I got rid of them all and I haven't needed any since.''

''Smart of you to turf them,'' said Liz; she'd made no secret of her dislike for Karyn's husband. ''How long's your lunch hour tomorrow?''

''Forty-five minutes max.''

''So that's out. I've got that wonderful sea-green dress I bought before Jared was born and that I've never been able to get into. It'd fit you.'' Liz sighed histrionically. ''You're so slim, just like I used to be.''

''It's not too dressy?''

''For Rafe Holden? No way. Can you come over now? And, Karyn, I can't tell you how happy I am that you're going out on a real date. The guy's a hunk—I've seen pictures of him. Just about made me salivate and I love my darling Pierre with all my heart.''

Panic flickering in her chest, Karyn rang off. An hour and a half later, she was home again. She hung the dress in her closet, taking a moment to admire it first. Liz had put the hem up an inch, but otherwise it had fit Karyn perfectly. She could wear the stiletto heels she'd bought on sale in town a couple of months ago because they made her ankles look so impossibly slim. Her mother had left her a pair of delicate crystal earrings that would be perfect with the dress; and in her precious forty-five-minute lunchbreak tomorrow she'd go to the drugstore for new eyeshadow and mascara.

And a new toothbrush?

She fingered the thin straps of Liz's dress. What was she doing, getting all dolled up to go out for dinner with a man wealthy beyond her imagining and so sexy he made her melt?

Playing with fire, for sure.

But hadn't Steve, in two years of marriage, crushed her

spirit of adventure? Dammit, she was going somewhere very special with an escort most women would die for, and she was going to have a good time. So what if she didn't have a clue exactly where they were going? So what if the next day she was back to eating macaroni and wearing work boots?

It'd be worth it, she thought, and went to have a shower.

Rafe was up early the next day. After breakfast he contacted his head office, swiftly delegating a job he'd planned to look after himself. He spent the rest of the morning working on his laptop. That afternoon, he drove through Heddingley and took the most direct route to Stanhope. Searching from side to side, he soon saw what he'd suspected he'd find: the Harveys' red SUV parked outside a split-level house. Their name was printed on the mail box. He drew up beside an elderly woman determinedly speed-walking along the shoulder of the road. "Excuse me? Can you tell me if Steven Patterson used to live around here?"

If she thought it odd that he was inquiring about a dead man, she was puffing too hard to question him. "In the Cape Cod next to the Harveys," she gasped. "His widow—such a sweet girl—sold it very soon after he died and moved into Heddingley."

"Thanks," Rafe said with his best smile. "You're setting a great pace."

"Why are calories so easy to put on and so hard to get off? If you can explain that to me, young man, you'll go far."

Saluting her, Rafe pulled a U-turn and drove back toward Heddingley. Yesterday evening, Karyn had twice avoided passing Steve's house. Plus, he thought with a catch at his heart, the river that wound so placidly behind it.

He then drove past the veterinary clinic. He could have

gone in; in a place this size, Karyn's boss would undoubtedly have known Karyn's husband. Or he could have indulged in gossip at the local supermarket.

He didn't want to do either one. He wanted Karyn to tell him about her marriage, and the grief that had followed Steve's tragic death.

He'd phone the clinic, though, when he got back to his hotel, and ask to speak to Karyn's boss. Planning ahead was a strategy that had never done him any harm.

Even if Karyn did tell him about Steve tonight, he still had to bide his time, building a relationship step by step. No sudden moves. His passionate need of her leashed.

She was worth waiting for. With every moment he spent in her company, Rafe was more and more convinced that in some way that still eluded him, she was important to him.

Wasn't that why he was here?

CHAPTER SEVEN

KARYN was ready at quarter to six. As ready as she'd ever be. She started pacing up and down her bedroom, growing more and more nervous by the second. More and more convinced that what she'd called playing with fire was nothing but insanity.

Rafe Holden wasn't for her. In bed or out.

In all likelihood she was risking a repeat of the terrible mistake she'd made with Steve, by getting in over her head with a man she knew virtually nothing about. Was she out of her mind?

At three minutes to six, the doorbell rang. She jumped as though someone had shot off a gun in her ear, made an unnecessary adjustment to the neckline of her dress and walked carefully downstairs in her high heels.

But two steps from the bottom, Karyn stopped. She wasn't walking toward a firing squad. She was going out to dinner with Rafe Holden. Any number of women would vaccinate a thousand sheep for the privilege. So was she going to behave like a terrified ewe?

No way.

She straightened her shoulders, pasted a brilliant smile on her lips and opened the door.

''My God,'' said Rafe.

Her dress was a brief shimmer of sea-green over impossibly long legs. Her shoulders and arms were bare, her cleavage...don't go there, Rafe. At her lobes, tiny earrings shot flashes of colored fire; her lips were luscious curves of iridescent pink.

Uncertainty flickered across her face. "Too much eye-shadow? Lipstick on my teeth?"

"You're perfect," he said unsteadily. "The most beautiful woman I've ever seen."

Her smile was more natural. "Oh, sure."

"I'm telling you the truth," Rafe said in a raw voice.

He meant it. Karyn's jaw dropped. "It's only my friend Liz's dress and makeup from the Heddingley drugstore."

"I don't care what it is, you take my breath away—and that's the truth, too."

Hadn't he done the same to her? Her cheeks flushing a bright pink that had nothing to do with makeup, Karyn said, "You don't look too bad yourself. Heck, who am I kidding? You're gorgeous, you're sexy, you look good enough to eat."

"Any time," Rafe said.

Her flush deepened. His light gray suit was impeccably tailored; his blue shirt was teamed with an elegant silk tie. He could have graced the pages of any glossy magazine. Yet beneath his highly civilized garments, she was all too aware of his sheer physicality: his muscular body, broad-shouldered and narrow-hipped; his every move with a predator's grace and sleek economy.

Danger, her brain screamed.

Shut up, she thought in an intoxicating surge of rebellion. I've earned a night out. The last three years have been hell on wheels and why shouldn't I have a few hours of fun? She fluttered her mascaraed lashes at him. "Is the restaurant—wherever it is—ready for us?"

"It might be. I'm not sure I am."

"I'm a small town girl, Rafe. Nothing fancy. Certainly not what you're used to."

Not like Celine, he thought. "Besides being so beautiful you knock my socks off, you're real, Karyn," he said forcefully. ''You've got integrity and courage. If you made a promise, you'd do your best to keep it. Don't ask me how I know that, I just do.''

''Well, of course I would,'' she said, slightly offended that he could even question that.

His voice deepened. ''If I kiss you, will I wreck that shiny lipstick?''

''According to the label, it's kissproof.''

''Why don't we put it to the test?''

Her breath caught in her throat. She closed her eyes, feeling his breath warm on her cheek, then the first tantalizing sweep of his mouth over hers. As her lips parted to the dart of his tongue, nothing could have stopped her low purr of pleasure. She locked her arms around his neck, lipstick and their destination dropping from her mind as he tasted and sought and explored.

He was clasping her by the hips, pressing her to his body; she could be in no doubt that he wanted her. In a thrill of pride, she allowed her own needs to surface, hot and urgent. Was this the adventure she craved? All her doubts and fears eclipsed in Rafe's arms?

It was Rafe who pulled back. With a hand whose tremor he couldn't quite disguise, he brushed a gleaming tendril of hair back from her cheek; then, briefly, buried his face in the sweet-scented curve of her shoulder. Bide your time, Rafe. Take it slow.

Easy enough to say, not so easy to do after a kiss that had made nonsense of his own counsel. ''We'd better go,'' he muttered, ''or we won't be going anywhere.''

''I have to relay every detail of the menu to Liz,'' Karyn said faintly. ''She'd never forgive me if I only took this dress up to bed with you.''

''A terrible waste,'' he said with a wry grin. ''Is that your shawl? It could turn cool later on.''

As she nodded, he picked up a white shawl woven from the finest of wool and threaded with silver. He draped it around her shoulders, his fingers brushing the smooth ivory of her skin. Bide your time, don't rush and keep your cards close to your chest, he thought crazily. All he had to do was follow his own advice.

All? It sounded like one hell of a lot.

Outside her house a shiny black limousine was parked, a uniformed chauffeur at the wheel. Karyn blinked. "Are you trying to impress me? Because if you are, it's working."

"We only go this way once."

Rafe helped her into the back seat, trying not to stare at her slim legs in their glistening hose. Then he got in the other side. On the seat between them was a great sheaf of pink roses. Karyn lifted them, breathing deep of their fragrance. "Are those for me?"

Her face was rapt, the voluptuous softness of her lips almost more than he could bear. He said clumsily, "If you want them."

"How could I not? They're gorgeous!"

She gave him a radiant smile, her eyes sparkling like the crystals at her lobes. Any sensible thoughts fled from Rafe's brain. "How was your day?" he asked with a singular lack of originality.

She began describing the various cats, dogs and pigs that she'd seen since eight o'clock that morning, and gradually he relaxed. When the limo came to a halt, Karyn looked out. "We're at the airport," she said, puzzled.

"That's my private jet over there."

A shadow crossed her face. "Where are we going, Rafe?"

"An hour's flight, to a resort I own in Maine. I'll have you home in time for work tomorrow."

Trust me. That was the message. Perhaps she could trust him; it was herself she was worried about. Rafe added, "You'll like it there, I promise."

She said with a frown that charmed him, "You're really very rich, aren't you?"

"Very."

"How many resorts do you own?"

"A couple of hundred."

"And how many houses?"

She looked as suspicious as though owning foreign property was a criminal activity. He said meekly, "The stone house in Droverton, a penthouse in London and the cottage in the Hebrides. A ski chalet in St. Moritz. And a lovely open bungalow in the Caicos Islands. But I spend as much time as I can at Stoneriggs, and I often loan the others out to friends."

"We've got nothing in common!"

"Karyn," Rafe said with sudden authority, "we're not getting into any heavy-duty discussions before dinner. If you leave money out of the equation, we've got a whole lot in common. The pilot's waiting for us—let's go."

The sleek Learjet delighted Karyn with its deep leather seats, kitchenette and fully appointed bathroom. Laying her roses carefully on an empty seat, she put her small overnight bag in the overhead bin and settled down to enjoy herself.

The resort was on an emerald-green island off the coast of Maine, private yachts and cabin cruisers dotting a sea smooth as glass. As the jet descended, Rafe said, "I've designed this place as a conference centre for executives. So there's a helicopter pad, meeting rooms with state-of-the-art technology and a sportsclub. You can see the marina from the air. There's also an Olympic-size pool in the solarium."

Karyn grinned. "I'd find it awfully difficult to concentrate on business."

"It's been a good investment," Rafe said casually, as the jet touched down and taxied along the runway, coming to a halt near a manicured golf course. Another limo was waiting for them on the tarmac. They drove along a winding road edged with fir trees and silver birch, past chalets tucked among the trees, and gleaming sand beaches interspersed with great chunks of granite. The main lodge, built Adirondack-style out of stone and cedar, took Karyn's breath away. But the limo kept going, until they reached a secluded cedar bungalow surrounded on three sides by magnificent copper beeches, dense shrubbery and gardens scented with lilies, honeysuckle and roses. The other side was open to the ocean and a curve of pale sand.

As they got out, Rafe said easily, "There are three bedrooms, choose whichever one you want. Then we'll go for dinner at the lodge."

Each bedroom had its own balcony, a fireplace, and a marble bathroom with a whirlpool tub and piles of luxuriously thick towels. In the living room, paneled in bleached pine, hand-woven rugs were scattered over the hardwood floor; modernistic glass sculptures framed a stone hearth. Karyn had run out of superlatives; she had no idea how she was going to describe all this to Liz. Perhaps it would be easier to tell Fiona, who was used to this kind of luxury.

Feeling as though she was in a dream, she walked with Rafe to the lodge under a sky blazoned with gold-flecked clouds. As they were greeted in the vaulted foyer with its expanse of windows overlooking the surf, Rafe glanced sideways at his companion. She looked as composed as though she visited resorts like this every day of the week, he thought with a quiver of amusement. After they'd been seated at their table and left with the menus, Rafe said softly, "You're not to even look at the prices, Karyn, have you got that?"

Trying not to gape at the high timbered ceiling, priceless carpets and even more priceless view, Karyn picked up the menu and opened the embossed leather cover. "I'm hungry enough to reduce you to penury," she smiled. Then, in spite of herself, her eyes widened in shock. "Rafe—it'll be bankruptcy."

"I own the place, remember? Order whatever you want."

This time her smile was pure mischief. "We won't end up washing dishes?"

"Not tonight."

She gave a sigh of pleasure. "How am I ever going to decide?"

Celine, he remembered, had taken for granted everything he'd given her. But Karyn wouldn't. Any woman capable of medicating a sick bull wasn't going to be blasé about the finest gourmet cuisine.

Was he falling in love with her?

He began discussing the appetizers, steering away from a question he wasn't ready to answer. When their wine was poured, he raised his glass. "Shall we toast Fiona and John?"

"To their happiness," Karyn said, sudden tears shimmering in her eyes. "I really miss her…and I'm dying to meet John."

"You can stay at Stoneriggs any time you like. Use it as a base."

Her lashes flickered. It was on the tip of her tongue to say he was taking a lot for granted; but hadn't he warned her against heavy-duty discussions? Savoring the chardonnay on her tongue, she exclaimed, "I've never tasted anything so wonderful—who else can we toast?"

He laughed. "Your friend Liz?"

"Absolutely. To Liz and Pierre."

He clinked his glass with hers. "I'm so happy to be here with you, Karyn."

The words had come out before he could censor them. Her blue eyes, deep and unreadable, flicked to his and then away. "I'll take that as a compliment to my borrowed dress."

It was, very subtly, a brush-off. Rafe felt the stirrings of anger, and stamped them down. A confrontation was no doubt in the offing. But he had no intention of it taking place here. "So you should," he said easily. "Why don't we toast my parents next? To Joan and Reginald—who are as madly in love now as they were when they got married."

She echoed him, the wine sliding down her throat. She didn't want to discuss the institution of marriage as embodied in his parents. "They run the castle, don't they?"

"In their eccentric way, yes." He began describing Holden Castle as it was many years ago and now, moving to his mother's pack of irresponsible dogs and his father's obsession with contract bridge. His face was lit with an affection that touched her in spite of herself. How could she not be drawn to a man who so unselfconsciously loved his wacky-sounding parents?

As the wine sank in the bottle, she began to talk about her own parents, her father's long battle with heart disease and the hardships that had brought to the family; her mother's steadfast support of husband and daughter. "I buried myself in my books at university—how could I not when she'd given up so much to send me there?" she said, taking her first mouthful of a leafy green salad lightly tossed with a cranberry vinaigrette. "Mmm…luscious."

"They use local ingredients as much as possible." Rafe asked another question, drawing her out about her childhood and adolescence. A shrimp terrine, scallops from the bay with julienned garden vegetables, and a maple syrup mousse followed, each accompanied by the appropriate wine. But even then, Karyn's tongue didn't loosen in one particular area: when he mentioned Steve's name once or twice, she swiftly changed the subject.

His hope that she'd share some of the details of her marriage wasn't panning out. He could have been more direct, insisting on answers to specific questions. But he wasn't ready to be quite so unsubtle.

As she drained her espresso, Karyn gave a sigh of repletion. "That was the best meal I've eaten in my entire life," she said. "Thank you, Rafe."

"My pleasure," he said, the simple words invested with new meaning. "Want to wander around the grounds for a while before we head back? Or dance on the patio?"

"I used to love to dance," she said wistfully. Steve had been a technically perfect dancer; but the music had never entered his soul, and she'd soon learned not to take other partners. Briefly a memory of his savage temper rippled along her nerves; she shivered, her eyes downcast.

"Are you cold?"

"Too much wine," she said with a smile that didn't quite reach her eyes.

"Let's go dance," Rafe said. All evening he'd had the sense that someone else was sitting at the table with them: a man called Steve, who'd died a hero. It was a feeling he could do without, he thought, getting to his feet and offering her his arm.

The canopied patio was entwined with wisteria, the blooms like ghostly blue lanterns in the moonlight. Several other couples were circling the floor to music that was dreamy and romantic; Karyn gave herself over to it, moving into Rafe's arms as naturally as if she'd been dancing with him all her life. He said, smiling down at her, "You're taller than you were in your steel-toed boots."

She chuckled. "Actually, my feet are killing me. How do women ever walk in these shoes?"

"Take 'em off."

Scandalized, she said, "Here?"

"Darling Karyn, we can make our own rules."

Darling...and was it true? Could she make her own rules? If so, she wanted the evening to end with Rafe in her bed. Once he'd taken her home tomorrow, he'd be leaving for Toronto, so what could be the harm? He'd told her back in England that he'd sworn off passionate relationships; so he wouldn't want commitment any more than she did. They could go to bed together and then go their separate ways.

The perfect ending to a perfect evening.

She leaned into Rafe's body, intuitively following his lead, feeling fluid in his arms, slumberous with desire. Lifting her lips to his throat, she whispered, "We could go back to the bungalow."

He said huskily, "I think that's a fine idea."

Even his voice was perfect, she thought with a frisson down her spine. As deep and smooth as the amber-colored brandy he'd ordered after dinner. Her whole body a single ache of longing, she let him take her by the hand and lead her from the dance floor. Hand in hand, they walked back to the bungalow. As he unlocked the door and they went inside, Karyn said casually, "When are you flying to Toronto?"

"I'm in no hurry."

"I thought you had a sale to look after."

"I delegated it. Got the report late this afternoon, it doesn't look like the site suits our criteria."

A little edge to her voice, she said, "But you're going home soon."

"In a hurry to get rid of me?"

All her senses alert, she said with careful truth, "If we go to bed together tonight, it's not the start of an affair. Or of any kind of commitment."

Rafe said sharply, "You mean you'll spend the night with me providing I head across the Atlantic tomorrow morning?"

"You told me when you arrived that you were dropping in—not staying long, in other words."

"Maybe I've changed my mind."

"Maybe you should have communicated that to me." She gave a sigh of frustration. "Rafe, I don't want to end a magical evening by arguing with you. You said to me once that you'd sworn off passion for life…*she ripped the heart from my body* was how you put it. That's why you were thinking of marrying Fiona, who, to put it mildly, didn't turn your crank. But what's between you and me—if that's not passion, I don't know what to call it. So I've been going on the assumption that the last thing you'd want from me is any kind of commitment."

She'd found, unerringly, the weak point in his armor. "It's too soon to talk about the future," he said forcefully. "I just want to get to know you. To see if there's anything between us to build on."

"Build what?"

"You don't let up, do you?"

"Most people don't travel four thousand miles for a picnic!"

His eyes like gimlets, he said, "I don't like talking about this—why for years even the thought of passion made me run a country mile. But it's time I did."

She said mutinously, "I don't need to hear your life story."

His voice dangerously soft, Rafe said, "Just listen to me for five minutes, will you?"

All Karyn's euphoria on the dance floor had vanished, eaten up by a pervading anxiety. "All right, I'll listen. But don't expect me to change my mind—I'm not into commitment."

"We'll get to the reasons for that later," Rafe said curtly, by sheer willpower forcing her to hold his gaze. "But this is about me. Why I was just fine until you came along." He paused, trying to calm down. When had he ever let a woman get to him as easily as Karyn did?

So much for his famous defences.

"I met Celine when I was twenty-five," he said, ironing any emotion from his tone. He was asking for understanding; not sympathy. "I was on the way up, living in high gear twenty-four hours a day. Working my guts out, traveling all over the world, dealing with men who had ten times my experience. Celine was from Paris, she was a model and so beautiful she stole my heart the first time I saw her." He moved his shoulders restlessly. "I figured she was unattainable. But to my intense gratification she wasn't. We fell into bed and for the next eighteen months I was head over heels in love with her."

Karyn stood still; through the open windows she could hear the shush of the breeze through the beech trees. She hated every word he was telling her. She was jealous, she thought incredulously, jealous of a woman Rafe had loved years ago.

Perhaps he still did.

"Celine traveled a lot with her job, as did I. But whenever we could meet, we did." Rafe grimaced. "Now I can see that the long-distance aspect was what made our affair last as long as it did, yet simultaneously destroyed it. The ending was predictable. I got home early from Bangkok and found her in bed with another man. Not the only man she'd been seeing, so I discovered when I confronted her. She'd been systematically betraying me from the beginning, all the while swearing her fidelity."

In the dim glow of light from the hall, his face was bleak. Karyn said gently, "I'm sorry."

"We all have to grow up sometime…but I'd trusted her. Completely. She laughed in my face, that was the worst of it. As though I'd been an utter fool to take her at her word. *But, Rafe, no one stays just with one man…how bourgeois.*"

"That was hateful of her," Karyn said hotly.

"After that night, I never saw her again. But from then on I only dated women who knew the score, and I kept all my defences in place. Like you," he finished sardonically, "I wasn't into commitment."

What was she supposed to say to that? "Lots of women are capable of fidelity."

"Fiona would have been, certainly. I knew her. I trusted her. I loved her in a way that didn't scare the hell out of me."

The words were out before Karyn could stop them. "Do you still love Celine?"

"No. It took a while, but eventually my feelings for her died."

"You don't love me."

Rafe winced inwardly. "I don't know what I feel. Other than straightforward lust."

"Do I scare the hell out of you?"

"Yes."

His monosyllable hung in the air between them. Karyn

said evenly, ''One more reason for you to fly straight home tomorrow.''

''And live like a coward for the rest of my life? I don't think so.'' He hesitated. ''I'm being as honest as I can when I say that marrying Fiona would have suited me in other ways. You see, I was ready to settle down. Spend more time at Stoneriggs, and raise a family. Fiona's always liked the idea of having children. It all fit together.'' He hesitated again. ''I still want to settle down and have a couple of kids. Just not with Fiona.''

A cold fist was squeezing Karyn's heart. She said quietly, ''There must be lots of women who'd be very happy to be your wife and the mother of your children. Go home and find one, Rafe.''

''I can't do that. Not when I'm beginning to think you're the one I want.''

''That's ridiculous! We've scarcely spent any time together, and the circumstances have been so complicated—you don't know anything about me.''

Some things you know from the beginning? She sure didn't want to hear that. ''You're forgetting something. I know Fiona. So in a way I know you.''

''My life's been completely different from Fiona's!''

''Why don't you tell me how? Not the money, not your career—the rest of it.''

She bent to undo the straps of her shoes, her dress glimmering softly, her cleavage shadowed; her shawl was a ghostly white. ''Let's cut to the chase. You're asking for intimacy. I don't do intimacy. I don't do long-term. Get that through your head.''

''Why don't you?''

''Because it hurts too much.'' She was telling the truth, she told herself fiercely. Well, sort of. It had just hurt in a different way than anyone else realized.

Rafe gazed at her in silence, his nerves stretched tight. She was talking about Steve. About a pain so deep that a year later she wouldn't even consider getting involved with another man. "You're the one who suggested we cut to the chase, Karyn," he said evenly. "Talk to me about Steve...how you met and what he meant to you. I don't have any idea what he was like."

"I want to go to bed with you. Not wallow in reminiscences."

"You're a widow, for Pete's sake! Why wouldn't I ask about your husband?"

She tilted her chin stubbornly. "I don't want to—there's no point. Rafe, we both know what happens when you and I get within ten feet of each other—and there's nothing wrong with lust. But I'm not going to dress it up as something it isn't. We can go to bed together and you can leave for England in the morning. Or we'll sleep in separate rooms."

"You want us to make love and then act as though it never happened."

"That's right." Suddenly she reached out, laying her hand on his sleeve and speaking with passionate intensity. "I want to be naked in my bed with you naked beside me. I want to taste every inch of you, I want to be held, I want you inside me." Her voice broke. "But that's all I want—I can't be any more honest than that."

His whole body felt as though it had been streaked with fire. He looked down at her slender fingers, feeling the pressure of her nails and imagining them digging into his bare back, the softness of her breasts against his chest, her long legs wrapped around his thighs. His heart was thudding against his rib cage. Wasn't that what he wanted, too? Karyn, naked and willing in his arms? The whole night before them...

With an effort that felt monumental, he pulled back. "But tomorrow you want me to get in my jet, fly back to England and stay there."

She nodded. "I'm on the pill, so I won't get pregnant. There'll be nothing to tie us together—and that's just the way I want it."

He said flatly, "I've been insulted a few times in my life, but you take the cake."

"You'd rather we didn't use protection?"

"I'd rather you didn't treat me like a one-night stand!"

Her nostrils flared. "Sex without commitment—men have been doing it for years. But I'm not allowed to because I'm a woman?"

"Clever, Karyn. This isn't about equal rights—it's about caring and intimacy."

"It's about relationship. We don't have one. I don't want one."

"Then I'm not going near your bed. Now or ever."

"Fine!" she snapped, clutching her shoes to her chest. "Sleep well and don't bother dropping in on me again." Then she stalked across the room to the farthest bedroom and slammed the door. The lock turned with an aggressive *click.*

Feeling as though he'd just done ten rounds with a champion heavyweight, Rafe left the bungalow and marched back to the lodge.

A woman he lusted after had offered him a night in her bed and he'd turned her down flat.

He was a fool. An idiot.

Be damned if he'd make love with her all night and then fly home in the morning as though nothing had happened. He wasn't going to be treated that way—discounted as though he could offer nothing but physical release. If that's all she thought of him, to hell with her.

Systematically Rafe went through the highly colorful stock of swearwords he'd learned in the many corners of the world. He didn't feel one bit better afterward. He told himself Karyn was just a woman: pretty, sure; sexy undeniably; but replaceable. How long was it since he'd gone to bed with anyone? Too long, obviously.

He'd be a fool to fall in love with her.

So he wouldn't.

First thing tomorrow he'd tell the pilot to prepare for a transatlantic flight. There'd be no hanging around in Charlottetown.

He'd soon find someone to settle down with, to be the mother of his children. He could advertise, Rafe thought cynically. They'd be flocking after him. Him and his fortune.

Karyn didn't care one whit about his money.

Karyn didn't care about him. Period. All she wanted to do was use him for her own ends and then cast him aside.

She was honest about it, though, a little voice insinuated in his ear. After all, isn't that how you've been living your life for the last six years? Ever since Celine took your pride and trampled it on a Paris street?

It wasn't the same thing at all.

No? Think about it, Rafe.

Scowling, he crossed the lobby, heading straight for the bar. He sat down, got the bartender's attention and ordered a brandy.

When it came, he stared at it moodily. He didn't want anything more to drink. Cupping the glass in his palm, he swirled the liquid around and around. Wasn't that what he was doing—going around in circles?

He was through with Karyn and her little games. He'd see her at Fiona's wedding, and no doubt at the christenings that in due time would follow. But he could handle that. By then, he'd be married himself.

"Buy me a drink?"

His head swiveled around. A very pretty young woman in a black dress had slithered onto the stool next to his. Daughter of a CEO, he thought. No harm in her, out for a good time and she'd picked on him. So, he thought ironically, he'd been presented with Karyn's replacement sooner than he'd expected.

"Sorry," he said, feeling old enough to be her father, "I'm not available. You should be careful who you come onto—not everyone's harmless like me."

"You don't look harmless."

He nodded at the bartender, tossed a bill on the counter and said crisply, "Serve the lady the drink of her choice and keep the change." He gave her a cool smile. "Good night," he said and strode out of the bar.

I'm not available. That's what he'd said.

As he approached the bungalow, he stopped for a few minutes under the shadows of the beech trees. To be unavailable was to be committed. He was committed to Karyn, a woman of undoubted passion who'd freed his own deep needs.

He didn't understand what that commitment meant. But it wasn't to be taken lightly.

He'd bet Holden Castle and his beloved Stoneriggs that Karyn was afraid to fall in love again. She'd done so once, and lost the man she'd loved. Who could blame her if she didn't want commitment? He himself had avoided it for years after Celine had dumped him.

Why should Karyn be any different?

Loosening his tie and shrugging off his jacket, Rafe headed toward the bungalow. He knew exactly what he was going to do.

CHAPTER EIGHT

A HALF-MOON silvered the trees and shrubbery, the lawns like a black carpet; except for a light in the hallway, the bungalow was in darkness. The soft plash of surf was the only sound. Rafe took a deep breath, inhaling the scents of newly mown grass and honeysuckle, laced with the tang of the sea.

What he was about to do would have long-lasting repercussions, he thought soberly. He was more than ready to allow passion back into his life, he'd proved that to himself the last few days. But he wasn't standing here in the dead of night just because he wanted to make love to Karyn. No, it was far more complex than that.

He wanted more from Karyn, a lot more; and he was willing to give more. To let down his defences and allow her in. To hope that eventually, if he were patient, she'd surmount her grief and do the same for him. Where that would all lead, he had no idea. Trying to ease the tension in his shoulders, he walked up the path toward the front door.

Somewhere inside the bungalow, Karyn screamed.

For a split second Rafe stood like a man transfixed, a chill racing the length of his spine. Then she screamed again, a choked sound wild with terror.

She'd locked her bedroom door. He couldn't get in that way.

He raced around the corner of the bungalow and in a great surge of relief saw that she'd left her bathroom window open. Leaping over the flowerbed, Rafe punched in the screen and levered himself over the sill. If someone was hurting her, he'd kill the bastard. Landing on his feet, he crossed the ceramic floor, not caring how much noise he made. The door to her bedroom was closed. He burst in, his fists at the ready.

Karyn was alone in the room. Sprawled facedown on the bed, she was whimpering in her sleep, breathing hard as though she were running. Even as he watched, she flipped over on her back, her eyes tight shut, her face contorted in an agony of fear.

Swiftly Rafe crossed the room and sat down on the bed. "Karyn, wake up—you're having a bad dream," he said, taking her by the shoulders and gently shaking her.

Her eyes flew open, stark with terror. "Don't come near me—go away!" She struck out at Rafe, frantically twisting her body as she tried to pull free.

He said urgently, "It's Rafe—you're safe with me, Karyn...I won't let anyone hurt you."

He was still clasping her by the shoulders. She went very still in his hold. "Rafe?" she whispered.

He pulled her to his chest. "It's all right," he murmured. "You were having a nightmare, that's all."

She was trembling now, tiny shudders that lanced him to the heart. Stroking her back with all the tenderness at his command, he said, "Tell me about it, what was happening."

She burrowed her head into his sweater, her arms fastening around his ribs with desperate strength. She had to tell him; she could feel the words beating at her skull, desperate for release. "It's always the same dream," she faltered. "But this time it went further than it ever has. I was so frightened and—hold on to me, Rafe, please don't let go."

"I won't," he said; and at a deep level knew the words for a vow. Binding and inevitable.

"The dream's about Steve. It's always about Steve."

"About him drowning?"

She shivered. "If only it were that simple..."

"Tell me. It'll help if you share it with me."

Would it? Karyn had no way of knowing. But she couldn't bear to carry this load on her own any longer. "I—I'm running away from Steve, that's how it always starts," she gulped. "I've left him and I know I have to get away and hide somewhere or he'll find me. Track me down like a hunted animal. It's in a city, I don't know where and it doesn't matter. I'm running down these dark alleyways...there are men sleeping on the sidewalk, all bundled up in newspapers like so much garbage, and I jump over them and run for the next alley. The whole time I'm terrified out of my wits—I keep hearing footsteps behind me but when I look, there's no one there. My lungs hurt and I can hardly breathe and I don't know how much longer I can keep going. Then, finally, I come out into the open and see the river, the water smooth as oil."

Her breath hitched in her throat. "Steve's standing there. His clothes are wet, still muddy from the river, and I realize he didn't drown after all. He has a gun in his hand and he's pointing it at my heart. Just as he's squeezing the trigger—that's when I usually wake up."

Rafe sat very still, listening with growing horror. A marriage was being revealed to him, a marriage the very opposite of the idyllic love match he'd pictured. He said neutrally, "What was different about the dream tonight?"

"I couldn't wake up. I was frozen, paralyzed, praying for release. Still holding the gun, he started walking toward me, taking his time, not saying a word because there was nothing he needed to say. We both knew I was powerless to stop him no matter what he did—that's when you woke me up."

"Thank God I did wake you," Rafe said harshly.

Her arms tightened around him. "I—I don't understand why you're here."

"I went back to the lodge, cooled down and figured you were right—I *was* using a double standard about commitment, one for you and one for me. So I came to tell you so."

Her brain still flashing with nightmare images, Karyn could scarcely take in what he was saying. "Whatever the reason, thank heavens you came back."

She was holding him so hard he could scarcely breathe. Her nightgown was made of some slithery material that bared rather more than it covered; to his nostrils drifted the same sensually layered scent he remembered from their first kiss. He still wanted her. That was a given. But when had he last comforted a woman, held her with a tenderness that sought to make her burdens his own? Or listened to an outpouring of terror that had appalled him?

Never, he thought. "Tell me about Steve, Karyn. What he was really like."

Wasn't it time for her to break her vow of self-imposed silence? And who better to do that with than Rafe? "How did you get in my room?" she asked, trying to steady her breathing. "I locked the door."

"Through the screen in the bathroom window. It now has a big hole in it—I'll have fun explaining that to the staff."

Her giggle had a slight edge of hysteria. "He-man stuff."

"I heard you scream," Rafe said tersely. "I wasn't going to hang around waiting for you to unlock the bedroom door."

"What if it'd been a burglar?"

"I'd have flattened him first and asked questions afterward."

A little kernel of warmth curled around her heart. "I bet you would have...my throat feels kind of weird, I need a drink of water."

She was no longer trembling. Rafe eased back from her, smiling down at her in the semidarkness. "There are glasses in the kitchen, I'll only be a minute."

Karyn nodded, watching as he got up from the bed and left her room: a tall, rangy man with black hair and a body that entranced her. She got up and went into the bathroom, her gaze riveted to the ripped screen. After closing and latching the window, she walked over to the sink. She looked like a ghost, she thought dispassionately, all big eyes and pale cheeks. Turning on the cold tap, she scrubbed at her face, wishing she could as easily scrub away the past.

When she went back to the bedroom, Rafe was sitting on the bed, propped up against the pillows, looking very much at home. She took a long drink from the glass he held out to her and perched a couple of feet away from him on the mattress.

He said easily, looping an arm around her, "Come closer."

It was so easy to yield to him, to let her head fall to his shoulder, to burrow into it and feel her overstretched nerves relax. For now, she was safe.

Knowing she'd lose courage if she planned what she was about to say, Karyn plunged right in. "I should never have married Steve. We scarcely knew each other—it was a classic case of love at first sight. Only trouble is, no one told me that kind of love can be blind as a bat...well, that's not strictly true. My mother tried to warn me, and so did Liz. But I ignored them both."

Rafe's shirt was smooth under her cheek; the slow rhythm of his breathing was very comforting. "Steve was handsome. He was sexy and charming. Polished, sophisticated and ambitious—he was an accountant with an international firm. So he represented a wider world than the island where I'd grown up and gone to university and gotten my first job. Yet he was in love with me, ordinary Karyn Marshall from Heddingley, Prince Edward Island. I knew I was the luckiest woman in the world. We got a special licence, got married, had a honeymoon in Hawaii and then came home and broke the news."

She sighed. "Once we were settled, we threw a big party to celebrate our marriage. An old boyfriend—he was there with his wife—asked me to dance. We hadn't taken ten steps before Steve cut in and whirled me away. I remember thinking at the time how strong Steve was and how much he loved me—so much so, that he wouldn't want me dancing with anyone else...naive, wasn't I? You can probably guess the rest. I gradually realized that Steve was enormously possessive and pathologically jealous. I work mostly with men. I visit a lot of farms, where there are more men. And yes, I'd dated at university, why wouldn't I? He questioned me obsessively, he didn't want to let me out of his sight in my off-duty hours, and he soon let it be known he didn't approve of my friendship with Liz."

"So you had no one to confide in?"

Grateful that Rafe had so quickly understood her isolation, Karyn nodded. "I suppose Steve did love me, in his way. That's what's so frightening—how many guises love can take, not all of them pleasant."

"Did he hurt you? Physically, I mean?" Rafe asked, taking care to keep any emotion out of his voice.

"Very rarely—he didn't need to." She frowned. "It was so insidious, Rafe. At first I thought he was joking. *If you ever dance with Dave again, I'll break your neck.* But then I realized that it was no joke. He meant it. He was bigger than me, much stronger...and yes, I was afraid of him. Outwardly—to my mother, at the clinic—I kept up this huge front that we were a loving and happily married couple. But all the while I was trying desperately to figure out how to leave him.''

''Living a lie's one of the hardest things you can do.''

''Just ask me,'' she said unhappily. ''A foolproof way to leave Steve—that's all I wanted. I couldn't just disappear from the face of the earth, and he'd told me if I left him he'd track me down no matter where I went. Was I going to spend the rest of my life looking over my shoulder?''

''You'd have left him,'' Rafe said. ''Eventually.''

''Maybe,'' she said, unconvinced.

''There's no question of your courage.''

''But that's just it! You know why I still don't talk about him? Not even to Liz, who's my best friend. Or to Fiona, my very own sister. It's because I'm so ashamed. He turned me into someone I scarcely knew. A coward, who jumped if a shadow moved. A woman who kept trying to placate her husband, please him, keep everything smooth on the surface. It would have been funny if it hadn't been so awful. I couldn't make him happy, no matter what I did, or how much I circumscribed my life and my friendships. My self-esteem plummeted. I despised myself because I didn't dare tell him to go to hell, because I was too afraid to walk out my own front door and never come back.''

She let out her breath in a long sigh. ''Well, you got an earful there.''

''Karyn, you had good reason to be afraid. There's nothing to be ashamed of.''

''I hated the woman I'd become,'' she said in a low voice.

She was picking at the fringe on her bedspread, her head downbent. Rafe lifted her chin, looking straight into her eyes. ''Your dream is prophetic—you knew all along that Steve was capable of violence. So you were wise to be afraid of him, and sooner or later you'd have figured out a way to get clear of him. I know you would.''

Tears caught on her lashes, she mumbled, ''I wish I could believe you.''

''You have nothing to be ashamed of,'' he repeated forcibly.

She ducked her head still lower. ''Yes, I do. I haven't told you the worst. When the police came to the clinic and told me Steve had drowned in the river, do you know what I felt? Relief. As though a huge weight had been lifted from my shoulders. That's a terrible epitaph for a marriage.'' She gave an unsteady laugh. ''And then, of course, he was hailed as a hero in the community, and I had to go along with it. It was true—he did save Donny's life at the cost of his own. I've tried so hard to believe that he redeemed himself at the end.''

Rafe kept to himself his own conclusions: that Steve's ego had been so immense he couldn't have conceived he might drown in the river that ran behind his house. ''You've never told anyone any of this?''

''I couldn't bear to. It was so tawdry, so unconvincing—sure, he gave me a few bruises every now and then, but otherwise I had no evidence. Outwardly, Steve adored me. People used to tell me how lucky I was to have such a handsome husband who doted on me.'' She grimaced. ''I sold the house we'd lived in, I sold his car, and I changed my name back to Marshall. The whole village looked at me askance, but there was no way I could explain.''

''Maybe you should try telling Fiona, who loves you. Or your friend Liz. Now that you've told me.''

Karyn sat up, turning to face him. "I'm glad I've told you, Rafe," she said slowly. "Thank you for listening."

She looked heartbreakingly fragile in her pale gown, her skin with the sheen of ivory. He could see the jut of her breasts under the silky fabric, and felt his mouth go dry. But how could he possibly suggest they make love after everything she'd told him? "If you're okay, I'll go to my room now."

"Stay here with me."

"Karyn, I—"

"I don't want to be alone, Rafe."

"All right," he said slowly, "I'll stay. I can sleep in the armchair."

She grabbed him instinctively. "No! Here in bed with me. I need you close."

A test, Rafe thought wryly. Of restraint, self-control and willpower. Could he lie beside Karyn in the velvet darkness, hold her in his arms and only offer comfort?

Sure he could. If that's what she needed.

Besides, how could he even be thinking of making love to her now that he knew what a wasteland of fear and loneliness her marriage had been?

Karyn sank down on the bed and tugged at his sleeve. "Hold on to me, Rafe...please."

He pulled off his shoes and socks, and tossed his tie and belt on the chair. Lying beside her, he drew her into his arms, gently pressing her face into his shoulder. She felt as tense as a cornered animal. "You're safe," he murmured. "No one will ever hurt you while I'm around."

For a space of time that felt like forever to him, she lay still; he had no idea what she was thinking. Then she pulled away, gazing up at him in the darkness. "Rafe," she said unevenly, "I want you to make love to me."

He reared up on one elbow. He'd outfaced tycoons and

bluffed his way through cutthroat negotiations on which his whole future had depended; but a handful of words from Karyn and he was speechless.

Ducking her head, she blurted, ''I shouldn't have asked you—I'm sorry.''

''Karyn, I'm not hesitating because I don't want you,'' Rafe said forcibly. ''But are you sure this is the right time? You've just had a horrible nightmare and you're upset...''

''I want you, Rafe,'' she said in a low voice. ''Now.''

His heart overflowed with an emotion he couldn't even name. He said huskily, ''You're sure?''

''Yes.''

She looked as high-strung as a racehorse, by no means as certain as she was striving to sound. So it was up to him to bridge the gap between the terror that was Steve's legacy and the joy that could be his own gift.

Rafe reached out and drew her into his arms again, her soft curls tickling his chin as he began stroking the length of her spine, smoothly and rhythmically. ''We've got all the time in the world,'' he whispered, closing his eyes and allowing his senses to be saturated with her: her scent, her warmth, her beauty. He moved to her shoulders, rubbing the tension from them, feeling her gradually begin to relax.

She gave a tiny sigh of pleasure and lifted her face to be kissed. ''I feel as though I've never done this before,'' she said with a shaky laugh.

''We haven't. Not with each other.'' He bent to find her lips, their waiting softness sending a shaft of heat the length of his body. He stamped it down. This wasn't about him. With exquisite control he laved her lips with his tongue, nibbling them, teasing them open, then kissing her in a surge of tenderness. A kiss he wanted to go on forever, he thought dimly.

The first flick of her tongue sent another of those heated

flashes through every nerve. He ran his hands along the yielding curve of her back, let his palms span her ribs and drift to the ripe swell of hip. The satin of her gown tantalized him with its smooth flow; frustrated him because it hid from him her nudity. Need slammed through him. But he couldn't rush her. He mustn't.

Then she undid three buttons on his shirt, sliding her hand beneath it. He gasped involuntarily as she tugged at his chest hair, exploring the arc of rib and the hardness of his belly. Releasing her briefly, Rafe hauled his shirt off, and in a firestorm of desire felt her press her breasts to his bare skin. He took their firm ripeness in his palms and lowered his head; pushing her gown aside, he suckled her, tasting, lingering, caressing, all the while inflamed by her small moans of pleasure. Her head was thrown back. He trailed his mouth the length of her throat, skimming the shells of her ears, nipping her lobes. Then, fighting for restraint, he kissed her again.

She said jaggedly, ''Take off my gown, Rafe.''

Her eyes were like deep pools of darkness; as she rose to her knees, he slipped the gown over her head and let it fall to the bed. Her body was illumined in the pale glow of the moon, all flow and surrender. He said, scarcely trusting his voice, ''You're so beautiful, Karyn.''

Drawing her closer, he buried his face between her breasts, the rapid staccato of her heartbeat echoing in his ear. He held the whole world. All he had ever wanted or desired.

As her fingers ran through his hair, he shifted his head, tonguing the sweet rise of her flesh and flicking its tip to hardness. She was whispering his name, over and over, her eyes closed in ecstasy, her body arching backward. He slid his mouth down the tautness of her belly, grasping her by the hips and then touching her between the thighs. She was hot and wet; he almost lost control.

With his fingertips he found her center, watched her shudder in response, her face a blur of desire. Using all the skill at his command, he played with her until she was writhing and sobbing. Beneath his fingers, the throbbing gathered and spun out of control and with the harsh cry of a falcon as it plummets from the sky, she collapsed into his arms.

Her heart was thrumming against his rib cage. Her tiny puffs of breath warmed his bare skin. Then she muttered, "Thank you, Rafe…oh, thank you."

"You don't have to thank me," he said, and knew, instinctively, that for Steve her pleasure would never have been paramount. He, Rafe, was more than making love to her; he was exorcising a ghost. Hadn't he known that all along?

He held her, his heart pounding, his whole body craving its own release. Very slowly she raised her head, her breath still as rapid as if she'd been running. Then she kissed him, her teeth scraping his lips in deliberate seduction.

He couldn't take much more. "Don't you think we should go easy, you must be worn-out—"

She was sinking down on the bed, fumbling for the catch on his trousers. "It's not fair," she whispered, "I haven't got a stitch on, and look at you." She gave a tiny, incredulous laugh. "Just look at you," she repeated, her eyes wandering over his body like licks of fire. "You're beautiful, too."

A simple compliment, yet it speared him to the heart. "Karyn," he said helplessly, "all I want is for you to be happy…"

She was edging his zipper down, her tongue caught between her teeth in concentration; suddenly impatient, he twisted off his trousers and his boxers. Since he'd first started massaging her shoulders, he'd been hard and ready for her; and had kept his distance, not wanting to frighten her.

She smiled at him, a smile of such sweetness that his breath caught in his throat. "I want you to be happy, too."

"I am," said Rafe, his laugh exultant. "How could I not be? I'm in bed with the most beautiful woman in the world."

"Come off it! What about Celine?"

He didn't want to talk about Celine; her many infidelities and the aftermath of her betrayal were past history. Over and done with. In a way, hadn't she done him a good turn over the years by keeping him single until Karyn erupted into his life? "Her beauty was on the surface," he said. "Yours goes all the way to your soul."

Karyn said unsteadily, "That's the loveliest thing anyone's ever said to me."

"Hang around," he teased.

Something flickered across her face. Then she said with an assertiveness that charmed him, "Kiss me, Rafe."

"Anything to oblige."

He eased her down to lie beside him, face to face, kissing her with an intensity that battered at his control. As he fought to hold fast to it, she caught his lower lip in her teeth, gently nibbling, each tiny sensual bite driving him closer to the brink. When she wrapped her arms around his waist and rubbed the whole length of her body against his, he couldn't hold on any longer. Imploding with desire, careless of his own strength, Rafe flipped her on her back and covered her, plunging to find her mouth.

And saw, briefly but unmistakably, the flick of remembered fear on her face.

It was gone before he could say anything; before he

could even draw back. Her eyes fathoms deep, Karyn took his face in her hands and kissed him with a kind of passionate desperation.

How could she ever have doubted her own courage, he wondered. Overwhelmed by sensations utterly new to him, Rafe kissed her back, his one desire to give her a depth of pleasure that would make nonsense of the past. Their tongues danced. Their hands roamed and caressed and explored; thigh was intertwined with thigh, hip held to hip. Their breath, ever more and more heated, mingled. Yet still he held back.

It was she who drew his hand to the damp heat between her thighs, who begged him, her head thrown back, ''Rafe, I need you inside me...I can't wait any longer. Oh God, Rafe, now...''

With exquisite care he parted the wet petals of her flesh and eased inside her. His face convulsed as she tightened around him, need coursing like a jolt of electricity through his frame. ''I can't—'' he began, and heard her cry out his name as the inner throbbing caught her and tossed her as though she was boneless, weightless.

It was all Rafe needed. He allowed himself to rise to the crest, heat and urgency lifting him until he could bear it no longer. His release was fast and tumultuous; his own cry hoarse in his ears.

His breath sobbing in his chest, he rolled over so she was lying on top of him, and held her tightly, his face buried in her neck. Beyond words. Beyond thought. Beyond anything but a storm of gratitude that he had found her: his mate, his beloved.

Beloved, he thought blankly, the truth hitting him between the eyes: a truth he'd been fighting for weeks. He loved Karyn, of course he did. Hadn't every second he'd spent with her since that first incendiary kiss in the woods been leading inevitably to this moment?

He was bound to her with a love as deep as the ocean, as wild as the fells. His soul in her keeping.

But he couldn't tell her so. Not yet.

Then, from a long way away, he became aware of the cool slide of tears on his shoulder. "Karyn?" he said hoarsely. "Did I hurt you?"

She was crying in earnest now, her slender body shuddering in his arms. Helpless to do anything but hold her, Rafe waited until her storm of weeping subsided. He reached with one hand for a tissue from the bedside table, pressing it into her palm. "What's wrong? If I hurt you, I'm more sorry than I can say."

Her breath caught in a hiccup. "You didn't hurt me—you were wonderful. More than I'd ever dreamed. I'm just so—Steve was the only man I'd ever gone to bed with, so I didn't know—"

"You mean you were a virgin when you married him?" Rafe asked with careful restraint.

"I was brought up with strict standards, and in university I was too busy studying to fall in love. So Steve was the first and only one until tonight…it somehow never worked with him, I never felt—I don't even know how to say it." She scrubbed at her eyes. "He used to blame me, saying I was too uptight, and of course the more he blamed me the more uptight I got. I—I just never realized what it could be like."

Her eyes downcast, she plucked at the hairs on Rafe's chest. "You must think I'm an awful—"

"I think you're the bravest woman I've ever met, as well as the most beautiful."

She lifted her head, tears still streaking her cheeks. "You mean it, don't you?"

"Yes. Every word." He longed to tell her how much he loved her; and with every vestige of his self-control, held back. It was too soon. She wasn't ready.

"I really want to believe you. I can't tell you how much I want to."

"You will. Soon."

Again her cheek fell to his chest. Her eyes drooped shut. "I'll work on it," she said, and within moments her breathing slowed and deepened.

Rafe lay still, staring at the shadows on the ceiling. The small hesitancies in her love-making, the dazzled smile when he'd teased her nipples to hardness, the shocked gasp when he'd first brought her to climax: they all made sense now.

He couldn't think of a word harsh enough for the man she had, in all innocence, married.

He was going to get her away from Heddingley for more than one night, he thought. Away from the river and the Cape Cod house. Away from Donny and Donny's parents and all her memories. To a place where he could tell her how much he loved her.

How was he going to do it, and where would he take her?

Within two minutes, a plan fell neatly into his mind.

CHAPTER NINE

"I'VE NEVER seen anything this beautiful in my life, Rafe. The blue—it's so intense, so dazzling."

"The color of your eyes," Rafe said.

Karyn smiled at him uncertainly. "How did I end up here? Yesterday morning I was in Maine, and today I'm in this utterly gorgeous place—when you pull strings, you pull them hard."

"Gets results," he said. He'd pulled them hard because he'd been afraid that, given time to think, Karyn might not fall in with his plan. "Your boss told me he was happy to give you the time off, and I bet you'd rather be here than at the clinic."

"I'm not that addicted to my job. But I'm still not quite sure why I agreed to this."

"Because you wanted to. Because you haven't traveled much. Because I was very persuasive."

"Right on all counts...especially the last."

She turned back to the breathtaking azure of the Saronic Gulf, Cape Sounio a gray-green blur on the horizon. Waves lapped the shore; the sky was another shade of blue, cloudless and hot. A foreign sky, she thought with a tremor of excitement. A Greek sky. Hadn't she always wanted to come to Greece?

"You own this hotel just like you own the resort in Maine," she said, remembering the deference with which she'd been treated half an hour ago when she'd walked through the blindingly white archway of the Attica Resort. The whole place was luxurious beyond anything she could have dreamed. She and Rafe were staying in his personal suite, with its private outdoor swimming pool, its hedge of pines and olive trees that gave them an unassailable privacy. It boasted a patio trellised with grapevines, which overlooked the pool and the bay. All the rooms had tall windows, each opening onto a view more stupendous than the previous one, while the furnishings were modern, their hues complementing the outdoors, beckoning it within.

She had, quite simply, never seen anything like it.

She was going to enjoy every minute of her stay, she decided. No matter that Rafe had overridden all her objections to spending four days with him in a place of his choice. No matter that she'd been too excited to sleep on the overnight flight; or that her wardrobe—even including Liz's borrowed dress—seemed hopelessly inadequate. Her clothes, inadequate or otherwise, were already hanging in the walk-in closet in the spacious, cream-painted bedroom that she was, apparently, to share with Rafe.

She would make love with him again. Her nerves tingling, she wondered if their second love-making could possibly match their first, in a moonlit bedroom thousands of miles away.

Maybe it wouldn't. Maybe that had been a fluke.

"You look very serious," Rafe teased. "What are you thinking about?"

She blushed fierily. He looked very much at home in his white shirt and trousers, his feet bare, his black hair gleaming in the brilliant sun. Why not make love with him now and find out?

No one, other than Rafe, knew her here. The woman who'd gone underground in the months of her marriage could be allowed to surface here. To take all the risks and have all the fun that had been denied her for too long. Karyn gave a sudden ripple of laughter, kicked off her sandals and walked over to him, the boards hot under her soles. His eyes, a darker blue than any ocean, smiled down at her. She looped her arms around his neck, pulled his head down and kissed him very explicitly.

Lifting her off her feet, Rafe kissed her back, stunned by the hard, hot thrusts of her tongue. God, how he wanted her. The last twenty-four hours, until he could get her here, had felt like the longest in his whole life.

She whispered, pausing to nip at his lips, "Take me to bed, Rafe."

His answer was to sweep one arm under her knees and pick her up as though she weighed nothing. "I thought you'd never ask."

Her cheek against the crisp cotton of his shirt, she was carried across the dining room, through the elegant ease of the living room to the bedroom. The spread was a soft yellow; one window was shaded by a thicket of trees, the other open to the gulf and the Mediterranean sunshine. When he put her down by the bed, then stripped back the covers, she began, very slowly, to undo the row of tiny buttons that fastened the bodice of her green sundress.

Rafe stood still, watching her. Her face was flushed a delicate pink, her lips were parted and her hair was like spun gold. The dress slid from her shoulders, slipped to lie in a green pool on the floor. She was wearing nothing but silken panties, also green. Lifting one knee with a grace that cut him to the heart, she eased them down her legs. Then she leaned over and started to undo his shirt, her tongue caught between her teeth in concentration.

He reached for his belt, and within moments they were both naked. She closed the distance between them, her breasts brushing his chest, and went with her intuition. "You held back last time, didn't you?" As he nodded, she said with gathering conviction and a boldness that startled her, "I'm glad you did. I was frightened and you were so good to me, so gentle. But now I want more. Remember our first kiss, in the woods near Willowbend? I want that again. I want you to drive me out of my mind."

With brutal truth he said, "Just looking at you drives me out of my mind."

So she had that power…her blood pounding in her ears, Karyn lifted her face for a kiss that swept aside any lingering doubts she might have had. He was her lover, the man who'd reawoken her to passion. This time she wouldn't be afraid.

He pushed her back on the bed and straddled her, his body hovering over her as his mouth plummeted to find hers. Their lips fused, feverish and demanding, his teeth scraping her tongue. She locked her arms around his nape, devouring him, tasting him, savoring him. "I need to touch every inch of you," she gasped, her body arching to meet his; his chest hair abraded her breasts, inflaming every nerve she possessed. He fell on top of her, then rolled over so she was riding him; lifting both hands, he cupped her breasts, playing with their tips until she threw her head back in ecstasy, the light molten on her skin.

Then his fingers, those wondrously sensitive fingers, were tracing the curves of her waist, the rise of her hips, drifting, always drifting, closer and closer to the juncture of her thighs. She was almost sobbing with need by the time he touched her there; sensation after sensation ripped through her body until she couldn't hold back any longer. Shuddering, she fell into the tumult, her hands gripping his wrists as though she were drowning and they were all she could clasp.

Gradually she came back to herself; she wasn't drowning, she was achingly and brilliantly alive, at one with the blue of the sea and the sunshine streaming in the window.

Her breasts rising and falling with the pounding of her heart, she said softly, "You're the most generous of lovers. But now it's your turn…lie still."

She lowered herself to the mattress beside him, and gave herself over to a sensual haze of taste and touch. Exploring him. Learning him. Hearing, with that thrill of power, his gasps of pleasure, watching his features blur with desire. Her hands roamed lower, down the tautly muscled belly until she was circling the silken heat and hardness of that desire.

His face convulsed. With a suddenness that sent a fast jolt of excitement through her, he lifted her so that she was, again, riding him. Then he drove into her, into the wetness and slick warmth, into the welcome that was Karyn. The woman he loved.

The words, those three little words *I love you* that were so all-important, were on the very tip of his tongue. Rafe forced them back. Not yet. Not yet.

She was sliding up and down, gripping him, sharp cries of mingled pleasure and need rising in her throat. Deep within her, the drumbeat of her climax was rising, too, toward its inevitable crescendo; overwhelmed, Rafe let his own pounding rhythms meet hers and meld in simultaneous and explosive release.

Slowly Rafe came back to himself. Karyn was lying on top of him, her body damp with sweat. Against his chest he heard her say raggedly, "I've never in my life felt like that—I didn't know I could. Oh, Rafe, I don't think I can breathe. Let alone sit up."

Holding her close, he kissed her ear; her soft, sweetly scented curls were tickling his cheek. "You don't have to sit up. Breathing would be good, though."

How else, other than with humor, was he to defuse a lovemaking that had taken him to a place he'd never visited before? Every instinct was warning him against speaking his love. It was too soon; he risked frightening her off.

He had time. The next few days, to start with.

Minute by minute the days passed, each one convincing Karyn that she would never forget even a single second of this magical interlude. She and Rafe swam in the pool, lazed in the sun and ate delicious meals that appeared from nowhere and whose flavors were often new to her: *tsipoura, tzatziki, gemista.* Every day they agreed they should drive north into Athens, and see—at the very least—the Parthenon; and every day they delayed this outing once again.

On the second day, Karyn phoned Fiona. ''Guess where I am,'' she said.

''Somewhere with Rafe, I hope—he told me he was going to see you.''

''I'm lying by the pool at a gorgeous resort south of Athens.''

''I want all the details.''

Karyn laughed. ''Not quite all—I'd be arrested.''

''Are you trying to tell me you and Rafe are an item?''

''For now,'' Karyn said hastily.

''We all have to start somewhere. Karyn, I'm so glad—ever since I met you, I thought you and Rafe were made for each other.''

''You *did?* You never said so.''

''Thought it might scare you off. You're what you might call gun-shy.''

''Fiona, I'm ready to tell you about Steve now. Not on the phone—but the next time I see you.''

''You and Rafe should get together more often.'' Fiona's voice sobered. ''I'm always happy to listen to whatever you want to tell me.''

Rafe had just emerged from his office, where he spent

part of every morning working. Karyn watched him peel off his shirt and shorts and dive into the pool, as naked and beautiful as a Greek god. A thread of panic in her voice, she said, "This isn't permanent. Rafe and me, I mean."

"Nothing's permanent," Fiona said grandly. "Well, that's not true. My wedding plans are. Did I tell you..."

Ten minutes later, Karyn said, "I've got to go—Rafe wants me to join him in the pool. This is such a heavenly place, Fiona, I don't know how I'll go back to ordinary living."

"Perhaps you won't. Give my love to Rafe. And Karyn, I'm so glad you're happy."

"I am happy," Karyn said blankly. "You're right."

"Good," said Fiona. "Love you. Bye."

Suddenly frightened by just how happy she was, Karyn plunged into the pool and gave chase to Rafe. She spent that afternoon browsing in the hotel boutiques, driving her credit card to the limit with her purchase of a flowing pink silk nightgown; it very satisfactorily caused Rafe to abandon his computer the next morning to ravish her, once again, in their big bed.

Because, of course, that was the other thing they did. Make love. Day and night, she thought, with a secret smile of delight. The whole four days one long haze of sensuality.

Rafe said lazily, "You look like the kitchen cat when he finds fish in his bowl."

He was stretched out beside her under the trellis, where the grapes were ripening; sun and shadow dappled his body. "Fish? No way. Caviar," she said, letting her eyes run suggestively from his tanned shoulders to his narrow swim trunks.

"We're going dancing tonight in the ballroom—we should save some energy for that."

"Can't take the pace, Rafe?"

"Try me."

This time they made love under a screen of green leaves and blue sky; once again Rafe drove Karyn out of her mind with a desire so hot and sharp she wondered if she would survive it. When, finally, she lay back on the soft pillows, she muttered, "Dancing? Did you say dancing?"

"I did." In a lithe movement he got up from the lounger. "Come with me—I bought you something this morning. If it doesn't fit, it can be altered this afternoon."

She took his hand, following him into the bedroom. He opened the cupboard and took out a long evening gown, strapless, made of delphinium-blue raw silk.

"I saw that yesterday in one of the boutiques," she stammered. "I didn't dare try it on because I knew I couldn't afford it. Oh, Rafe, I adore it."

"It's yours."

Her instinctive protest died on her tongue. "To wear tonight?"

"With this," he said.

The rectangular box he was holding out was made of black leather embossed with gold. She said breathlessly, "You've given me so much already. These last four days..."

"Karyn, I make a lot of money. Let me enjoy spending a little of it on you."

"If I refuse, I'll sound ungracious."

"That's right...say, *Thank you, Rafe,* and try it on."

She pried the box open. A single teardrop diamond on a delicate gold chain was nestled into the white velvet lining. "Thank you, Rafe," she whispered and lifted it from the box with fingers that were trembling. "No one's ever given me anything so beautiful."

He took the chain from her, looped it around her neck and fastened it at her nape. Then he drew her over to the mirror, where she saw a naked woman still glowing from the act of love, the diamond sparkling like fire in the valley between her breasts.

Was that woman herself? She said faintly, ''I'll be proud to be your partner tonight,'' and knew she'd said just the right thing.

In the glorious ballroom, open on two sides to the gulf and a sky glittering with stars, Karyn danced until her feet hurt. At midnight the buffet was spread with a dazzling array of dishes, each like a work of art, the table decorated with pale pink orchids and ice sculptures that caught the light from the chandeliers. Rafe was punctilious about introducing her to the other guests and to some of his business associates; Karyn tried out her newly learned Greek and danced some more.

The whole evening she was aware of Rafe's body held to hers, of the electricity that lay just below the surface, waiting until they were alone to be ignited. His body language said, more clearly than words, that she was his. Yet when she danced with other men and Rafe with other women, she sensed he was comfortable with this in a way Steve had never been. She also knew he was only waiting for her to return to his arms.

Where she longed to be.

At two-thirty in the morning, they made a round of goodbyes and left the ballroom. As Rafe locked the door of their suite behind them, Karyn kicked off her high-heeled sandals. ''I hate to take the dress off,'' she said wistfully, ''I feel like a flower in it.''

''A very lovely flower,'' he said, and kissed her long and hard. The result was predictable; Rafe took off the dress for her, and they made languorous and overwhelmingly sensual love: one more of the many moods of passion. Afterward, Karyn stretched as gracefully as a cat. ''How many times was that today?''

Rafe laughed. "We both need to go home for a rest."

"Tomorrow," she pouted. "Back to reality. Yuk."

"We'll come again. Or go somewhere else. There are Holden Hotels all around the globe."

She didn't want to think about the future. Just the present. "I've had a wonderful time," she said impulsively. "I'm so grateful you brought me here."

"Gratitude goes both ways, Karyn."

He? Grateful to her? What for? "You own everything you could possibly need," she exclaimed. "Just look at what you've given me—how can I ever thank you?"

"By being yourself…that's all I ask."

She shifted restlessly. "How will it work tomorrow? Will I fly commercially from England to get back home?"

"No need for that—we'll use the jet. I'll go with you."

Her eyes widened, a shadow in their depths. "Why would you go with me?"

"Because I want to."

She lay still in the circle of his arms. In the last four days Karyn had learned considerably more about Rafe than the overpowering fascination his body held for her. There were the ordinary things: that he was an expert swimmer, he danced like a dream and his tennis backhand was a killer. He was well-versed in matters political, artistic and literary; their conversations entranced her, expanding her horizons. He treated the staff with an innate courtesy that she could only respect.

She'd learned something else: when he retreated to his office every day, his voice on the phone had a forceful edge, a decisiveness all the more powerful for being understated, that made her ill at ease for a reason she wasn't quite ready to examine.

Her eyes lingered on his hands, with their long, lean

fingers and strong wrists. She would miss him. Desperately. She'd have to get used to sleeping alone again; in the privacy of her own thoughts, she could admit how much she loved waking in the night and finding Rafe's arm lying heavy over her shoulders, or drawing her snug to his hips in sleep. But hadn't she known from the start that this was an interlude, beguiling and impermanent?

She didn't want him to come back with her to Heddingley. Far better that she make any adjustments on her own, in her own time. "I'll have to go back to work as soon as I get home," she said crisply.

"Then I'll cook supper for you," he drawled; because her head was bent, she didn't notice how sharply he was watching her. He reached over to the bedside table, where there was a tray of exquisitely prepared fruit, and passed her a sliver of mango. "It'll be a comedown from the meals here, I warn you."

The mango was ripe and slippery. Licking her fingers, Karyn said, "I'm not sure I like this conversation. All good things have to come to an end."

"Do they, Karyn?"

"Yes, they do," she announced. Suddenly exhausted, she kissed him in the vicinity of the chin and closed her eyes. While it might be perfectly clear to her that she didn't want Rafe coming to Heddingley, it was, after all, his personal jetplane; she could hardly kick him off it. Not when he'd been so overwhelmingly generous to her, and she owed him so much.

Once they got back to Heddingley, she'd insist that he leave right away, so that her life could settle back to normal. By no stretch of the imagination could normal include Rafe Holden.

He'd understand her point of view.

* * *

It was in London, as they waited for the jet to be refueled, that Karyn discovered Rafe wasn't interested in understanding her point of view. In fact, he didn't see eye to eye with her at all. He was sitting in the private lounge reading a Greek newspaper, its script incomprehensible to her. He was frowning. She said lightly, "Is the news that bad?"

He scarcely heard her. The headlines on the second page concerned an Italian businessman who had traveled to Athens and murdered his estranged wife there. The story sickened him; it could so easily have been Karyn.

She said patiently, "Rafe? Hello? Is anybody home?"

His lashes flickered. "Sorry. We won't be much longer. You can sleep all the way home if you want to."

Filled with confusion, she burst out, "I still don't understand why you're coming with me!"

"What did you expect me to do? Dump you at my earliest convenience?"

"Of course not," she said shortly. "But there's no point in you crossing the Atlantic when I have to go right back to work. This has been absolutely wonderful, and I can't thank you enough. But it's over now. There's no point in dragging it out."

"Is that how you see spending more time with me?" he said with menacing softness.

She bit her lip. "I have to pick up my normal life. I have a job, a house, friends and responsibilities—and so do you." Attempting to lighten the atmosphere, she added, "Several houses, in your case, and megaresponsibilities."

"And when—in this busy life of yours—will you find time to see me again?"

Her temper flared, driven more by nerves than actual anger. "Cut the sarcasm. I'll be in England for Fiona's wedding, I'll see you then."

"What if I want more than that?"

"You don't. So why are we fighting like this? The last thing I want to do is ruin a perfectly marvelous four days."

"How, all of a sudden, do you know what I want?"

His voice was tight with controlled anger. In an ugly uprush of emotion, all Karyn's old fears resurfaced. Steve had never been ready to let go of her: the more she'd given him, the more he'd demanded. Was Rafe the same?

Surely not. Not Rafe.

But no matter how hard she tried, she couldn't force her anxiety back where it belonged. Her own anger flared to match his. "Okay, so I don't know what you want. How about enlightening me?"

Rafe tossed the newspaper on the marble table and said in exasperation, "This is all wrong, Karyn. Trading cheap shots with each other like this."

She said flatly, "Tell me what you want. We'll go from there."

He gazed at her in silence. She was wearing simply cut linen pants and an embroidered vest she'd bought at the Athens airport. She didn't look conciliatory. Neither did she look at all like a woman in love. For a moment fear ripped through him, as imperative in its own way as desire. Thrusting it down, he said, "I want to keep on seeing you."

"Why?"

"We fit together. And I don't just mean sexually."

"We're great in bed. But other than that, we couldn't be more different. Look where we just stayed, Rafe! On my own, I couldn't afford that suite for four minutes, let alone four days."

"There's a lot more to me than my money."

"You're enormously rich. I'm a country vet. You travel the world while I drive from the pigsty at LeBlanc's Farm to the local stables. You're cultured and sophisticated. I've barely been off Prince Edward Island and half the time I'm covered in mud. Your lifestyle and mine, they're as different as—''

As she fumbled for an analogy, Rafe rapped, ''As I am from Steve. Because that's what this is really about, isn't it? It's not about money, it's about Steve.''

She stood up, jamming her hands in her pockets, determined not to cry. ''Of course it's about Steve. You're the only person in the world who knows what he did to me. How he changed me. And yet you expect me to keep on seeing you? To start some kind of relationship with you? You, of all people, should understand why I can't do that.''

She now sounded despairing rather than angry; again a deep unease spread through his body. ''Yes, you can,'' he said forcibly. ''You did tell me about him, that was a huge step—and I know you're going to tell Liz and Fiona. Since then, you've spent the better part of four days in bed with me. I'm going to sound arrogant as hell, but you liked making love with me—nobody can fake the way we were together. Wasn't that another giant step? In bed with me, you let yourself be the woman you really are.''

The force of his willpower battered at her defences; his eyes were a hard steel-blue. ''I can't risk getting close to you.''

''Dammit, you've been as close to me as you can get. In bed, in my arms.''

''That's not what I mean. That's just sex. Astounding and incredible sex. But still sex. I mean intimacy, real intimacy. The kind that hurts too much when it goes wrong.''

''You're assuming it's going to go wrong.''

''You say you're different from Steve. But you're also like him. Handsome, charismatic, sexy, from a wider world than my own, with more money. I fell for Steve lock, stock and barrel—and I've paid for that mistake ever since. I can't afford to get involved with you.'' Her voice rose. ''Why don't you understand?''

''Outwardly, maybe I am like Steve. But did you yell at him like you just yelled at me?''

She flinched. ''Initially, yes.''

''Are you afraid of me, Karyn?''

Her shoulders sagged. As usual, he'd gone to the heart of the matter. Choosing her words, she said, ''I'm afraid of what might happen if we continue seeing each other. You're a very powerful man—you wouldn't have risen to the top if you weren't. You're used to getting your own way. In business, and with women, I'm sure.'' Her smile was twisted. ''I don't imagine you get turned down very often.''

This time some of his anger escaped in his voice. ''You think I'm after you just because you're unwilling? That's how I get my kicks?''

''I didn't say that! All I'm saying is no. Two letters, one syllable, not a complicated word. No, I don't want you to come to Heddingley with me. No, I'm not interested in a relationship with you.''

''Because of Steve.''

''Because I lived in fear of my husband for months—a man I'd married for love.''

''We all have our nightmares.''

In deliberate challenge she said, ''What are yours, Rafe?''

''Realizing at age seven that my parents, for all their fine lineage, were dirt poor, and that I might be stuck in a moldering old castle for the rest of my days.''

''From which Douglas rescued you…is that all?''

''Going to boarding school and having the tar beaten out of me because word had gotten out that I didn't have two pennies to rub together. After that, I learned to fight dirty.''

''You still do,'' she said caustically.

''No, I don't—I don't need to.'' Briefly his jaw hardened. ''Celine was the one who fought dirty. Telling me she adored me and neglecting to mention she adored three other men at the same time. Now that's dirty.''

''Then for the next six years you avoided passion and intimacy—six years, Rafe! Steve drowned a year ago. Yet you want me to pretend it didn't happen?''

He said with fierce conviction, ''If I'd met you a year after I dumped Celine, I'd still be acting the way I'm acting right now.''

''I'm supposed to believe that?''

''Yes,'' he grated, ''you are. Look, I understand that my nightmares, bad as they were at the time, can't possibly compare with yours. I'll give you all the time you need. But in the meantime I have to be able to see you.''

''Rafe, I hate this! I can't do it. I won't.''

''Then Steve wins—is that what you want?''

''Of course he wins,'' she said wearily. ''His kind always does.''

''That doesn't have to be true—get to know me and see that I'm not like him at all.''

Rafe was gripping the back of the nearest chair, his knuckles bone-white with strain. Compassion ripped through her; but even that didn't—couldn't—change her mind. ''The only way you get to know someone is by living with him,'' she said in a low voice. ''I trusted the world until Steve came along. He destroyed every vestige of my innocence. My trust in men, of course. But even worse, my trust in myself, in my own judgment.''

''So are you going to stay alone for the rest of your life?''

She shivered. ''How can I answer that?''

Ruthlessly he drove his advantage. "Don't you want children? You'd make a wonderful mother."

Her face pinched, she whispered, "Yes, I'd like to have children. But not so much that I'll marry to get them."

He played his last card…what did he have to lose? "I want to marry you—you must have figured that out by now."

"You *what?*"

He glanced around the elegant, impersonal lounge with its aura of impermanence, of travelers passing through on their way to other destinations. "I'd hoped to tell you this in a more romantic setting," he said harshly. "I've fallen in love with you, you're the woman I want to spend the rest of my life with. Wife. Lover. Mother of my children. The whole deal."

She said the first thing that came to mind. "But you scarcely know me."

"I know you. Going to bed with you, spending the last four days with you, how could I not know you? Anyway, you're forgetting I've known Fiona all my life. Your identical twin, who had the courage to fall in love and fight for a new life. You've got that same courage, Karyn. You just have to find it and trust in it."

"I was married for twenty-three months to a man who made every day a living nightmare," Karyn said bitterly. "That's the difference between Fiona and me."

He was losing her, Rafe thought. Right in front of his eyes, Karyn was moving away from him. He'd never begged for anything in his life; but if ever he needed to, it was now. He said roughly, "Forget I said I want to marry you. Or that I've fallen in love with you. Dammit, we'll even stay away from the bedroom if that's what it takes. But just let me keep on seeing you—that's all I ask."

Tears stung her eyes. For a man of Rafe's pride to humble himself for her sake...how could she bear it? "I'm not the woman for you, Rafe. I can't give you what you want—I'm so sorry. We should never have gone away together. I swear I wasn't using you, it just didn't occur to me that you might fall in love with me. If I'd thought there was any chance of that, I'd never have agreed to going to Greece with you."

Naked honesty shone from the shimmering blue of her irises. She wasn't playing games with him, Rafe thought. She wasn't like that. "Give me time," he said in a voice he scarcely recognized as his own. "Let me prove I can give you all the freedom you need, and that I trust you utterly. But don't send me away."

"I have to." Her voice wavered. "I'm sorry, Rafe, I hate hurting you like this. But I can't love you the way you want me to. Far better to end this now than drag it out and cause you more pain. Please—don't come to Heddingley with me. Go back to England and forget about me. Please."

He had his answer, and it was no. Finally and irrefutably no. His one need to get out of the lounge and away from her without revealing the raw agony clamped around his heart, Rafe pushed himself upright and said with formal politeness, "I'll speak to the pilot. He'll take you to the Charlottetown airport. I'll stay in London, I have some business I can do there."

She'd won. Exhaustion settling on her shoulders like a dead weight, Karyn said with answering formality, "Thank you. Goodbye, Rafe." She didn't hold out her hand or try to kiss him; to touch him would have undercut the last remnants of her control.

He said, "Wait here, the pilot will come for you shortly." Looking around like a man unsure of his bearings, he picked up his leather briefcase from the marble table and marched out of the lounge. The door swished shut behind him.

Karyn sat down hard on the nearest chair. She couldn't cry now, not when an employee of Rafe's could walk in at any moment. She concentrated fiercely on her breathing, trying to loosen the tight bands of tension around her chest.

She was going home. Home was where she needed to be. Until then, all she had to do was concentrate on holding herself together.

Her little house, the birch trees, the weed-ridden garden…that was where she belonged.

CHAPTER TEN

HOME had subtly shifted while Karyn was in Greece with Rafe. It echoed with silence and with her self-imposed solitude. Rafe wasn't there with her to share her jokes, to argue about a political situation, to describe a painting he'd seen in Moscow or a sculpture in Florence. To offset this, she put the TV on for white noise, played a lot of raucous rock music and did her best to root out the weeds in her mother's garden.

He wasn't there in bed with her, either. Not when she lay down, or when she woke in the night reaching for him, or when her body tormented her with hungers only he could feed.

He didn't contact her, by e-mail, phone or letter. It was as though he'd dropped off the planet.

She'd told him, more or less, to do just that. She had no cause to complain.

At the clinic she worked like a woman possessed, taking on extra shifts and staying after office hours, ostensibly to bring her records up to date, in actuality because she didn't want to go home. At least there were other people at the clinic; and when they got too much, there were dogs and cats who didn't require intelligent conversation of her.

Her second evening home, Liz phoned. ''You got back yesterday, didn't you? Tell me all about your holiday—was it wonderful?''

''I'm not seeing Rafe again,'' Karyn blurted. ''Except at Fiona's wedding.'' Which now loomed as ominous as a herd of sick elephants.

''Whatever happened?''

Her tongue falling over the words, Karyn found herself pouring out an abbreviated version of her marriage. ''We can talk more about it some other time,'' she finished, her voice jagged. ''But you do understand why I can't keep on seeing Rafe.''

Liz said carefully, ''So you didn't enjoy yourself in Greece?''

''Of course I did, it was fantastic. But it was totally divorced from reality…Rafe and I are worlds apart and that's the way I'm going to keep it. I'll bring back your dress tomorrow, Liz. Just don't ask any questions, okay?''

Liz would have had to be stone-deaf not to hear the misery in her friend's voice; she changed the subject, invited Karyn for dinner and didn't mention Greece, Rafe or the pretty sea-green dress. That same day, Karyn boxed up the diamond pendant Rafe had given her and sent it by registered mail to Stoneriggs.

Lacking the courage to talk to Fiona by telephone, Karyn e-mailed her. It was a brief and chirpy note, saying she'd had an incredible holiday but she was back to her real life now.

Three days passed without a reply, Karyn each morning searching in vain among her new messages for one from her sister. On the fourth day she fired off another e-mail, chatting about the dogs and cats she'd been tending, and asking about John. Again, there was no response.

Surely, Karyn thought in despair, focusing on the screen as though she could conjure up the reply she sought, her breakup with Rafe wouldn't cause her to lose Fiona's love. Life couldn't be that cruel.

The next day was Saturday, Karyn's day off. She slept in, had a luxurious soak in the tub and made a fruit salad and pancakes for breakfast. The sun was shining; she could work in the garden all day. She should have been happy.

She wasn't.

She was upstairs cleaning her teeth when the doorbell rang. She glanced out of the window; a taxi was reversing from the driveway. Her heart gave a great lurch in her chest. Rafe, she thought. Who else would arrive by taxi other than him?

Oh, God, what would she say to him?

She looked down at herself: denim cutoffs, an old tank top and bare feet. She sure wasn't dressed for the Attica Resort. Taking a deep breath, she walked downstairs and pulled open the door.

Fiona was standing on the step, a small overnight bag in her hand.

Karyn's jaw dropped. "Fiona," she cried, "I—come in, I wasn't expecting to see you."

Then, in a jolt of pure terror, she realized Fiona didn't look at all happy to be here. Her sister looked—grim was the only word that came to mind. "Rafe," Karyn said faintly, the color draining from her face, "something's happened to Rafe." She grabbed Fiona by the wrist. "What's wrong? Is he okay?"

Fiona said coldly, "What do you care?"

"Don't, Fiona! Just tell me if he's all right—you've got to tell me!"

"Except for a broken heart, he's fine."

Karyn leaned back against the nearest wall, her breath escaping in a big whoosh. "You just took ten years off my life."

Fiona said slowly, "So you do love him..."

"I do not!"

"We'll see about that. In the meantime, lead me to your

kitchen and make me a very strong cup of tea along with two fried eggs and a mountain of toast."

Fiona looked, minimally, less unfriendly. Karyn said crisply, "You'd think England was just down the road the way you and Rafe zip back and forth. Without even bothering to phone. You don't get the tea unless I get a hug first."

"Huh," said Fiona. But she opened her arms, and Karyn fell into them.

Burying her nose in Fiona's shoulder, Karyn gulped, "You didn't answer my e-mails."

"I had no intention of answering them. You look awful—shadows under your eyes and you've lost five pounds."

"Six, actually. You look great…you've had your hair cut."

Fiona's hair now fell in soft waves to her shoulders. "I did. Mother's in a perpetual snit anyway, so what does one more thing matter?"

"It suits you. You look different somehow."

"More grown up, you mean."

There was indeed a new maturity in Fiona's bearing. "Here, sit down at the table," Karyn said, "and I'll put the kettle on. Did you sleep on the plane?"

"Like a baby." Fiona gave a smug smile. "I only have to think of John, and I forget all about being five miles high over a very large ocean."

Karyn took out the tea pot and the frying pan. As she cracked two eggs into the pan, she said, "I'm so happy to see you. But I don't understand why you're here."

"Breakfast first," Fiona said with impressive authority, and leaned over to undo her bag. "I brought swatches of the bridesmaid's fabrics with me, you can choose which color you'd prefer."

So as Fiona ate her way steadily through eggs, toast and jam, washed down with liberal quantities of inky tea, they talked fabrics, flowers, cake and the etiquette of a wedding where one set of parents was far from delighted with their child's choice. Finally, replete, Fiona sat back. "That's better," she said. "Now we'll get down to business. Rafe arrived back at Stoneriggs looking worse than my father the day his investments went belly-up. I poured some brandy into Rafe—well, the best part of a bottle, actually—and got the whole story out of him. He told me about kissing you in the woods, and spending four days in bed with you and—"

"Fiona..."

Fiona gave another of those smug smiles. "I'm not nearly as easily shocked as I used to be. Rafe's in love with you, Karyn. Madly in love. A total goner. Ever since you sent him packing—for reasons best known to yourself—he looks as though someone bashed him on the head with one of Father's concrete statues. I haven't seen him like that since that bitch Celine ran circles around him and no, I'm not quite ready to use that word in front of my mother yet."

"I didn't do anything to encourage Rafe."

"In the woods at Willowbend you kissed him back. You went to Maine with him and to Greece. Where you had, by all accounts, torrid sex on the floor, on the patio, in the pool and even, occasionally, in bed." As a hot blush surged up Karyn's cheeks, Fiona added, "It was very good brandy. It loosened his tongue big time. At least you're not indifferent to him."

"Maybe not. But that doesn't mean I have to keep on seeing him."

"You're a coward."

"When I married Steve, I made a horrendous mistake. I'm trying to learn from it, that's all."

Fiona shoved back her chair, leaning both hands on the table. "How dare you compare Rafe to Steve!"

Karen stood up too, glaring right back. "How can I not? Two handsome, sexy men who swept me off my feet—I'm damned if I'll marry Rafe."

"Let me tell you something. I've known Rafe all my life. We're neighbors, we're best friends, I know him through and through. I've seen him with his parents, his servants, his crofters, and his horses. He taught me how to climb trees and ride bareback and steal ripe raspberries from under the gardener's nose. He rescued kittens from being drowned, he set false trails in the fox hunts, he stood up for kids who were being bullied. Yet you dare compare him with a man who by all accounts was a thoroughly nasty piece of work?"

"I didn't—"

"You were smart to be afraid of Steve. God knows what he might have done had you tried to leave him. But to equate him with Rafe—don't you see how *stupid* that is? Rafe's solid, he's decent, I'd trust him with my life. Let me ask you something. Do you think Rafe's capable of murdering you?"

"Of course not!"

"Of hitting you?"

"No."

"Threatening you?"

Karyn said furiously, "He doesn't let up. He's relentless, he rides over me like a ten-ton truck."

"Answer the question."

"He's never threatened me," Karyn said sullenly.

"Then would you mind explaining to me how he's like Steve—who did hit you and threaten you? Who kept you in line because underneath it all you were terrified for your life?"

Put like that, it did sound ludicrous to have compared the two men. Karen bit her lip, her face strained and unhappy. "I don't trust my own judgment any more. Especially with men."

"Then rely on mine for a while. I adore Rafe. Do you think I'd adore him if he abused his power? He definitely has power, don't get me wrong. Huge power. But his staff adore him, too, and that's because he treats each and every one of them like a human being." She paused, her head tilted in thought. "Maybe it's because he grew up poorer than most of the local boys. Blue blood's all very well, but it doesn't put food on the table or fix the roof."

Karyn said grudgingly, "I guess you're right, Rafe hasn't let his power go to his head."

"Of course I'm right. Here's another question. How did your husband treat the waitresses when you went out for dinner?"

"Badly," Karyn said in a small voice.

"There you go."

"Rafe was lovely with the staff at the Attica. I noticed."

Fiona said more gently, "Look, I'm not belittling what happened to you in your marriage, Karyn. It must have been terrible, and of course you're afraid to trust your judgment. So I'm asking you to trust mine instead. Rafe's a good man, I'd take that to the bank—and as for you and me, we're identical twins. If I trust Rafe—and I'd trust him with my life—then so can you."

"I don't know how! I don't know where to begin."

"Then I'll tell you something else. I've had to fight for my relationship with John, tooth and nail. Now that I'm in love with him, I'm freeing myself from my parents, from a lifetime of being—oh, ever so lovingly—crushed and controlled. I've been frightened sometimes, but I knew I couldn't back down or I'd be lost."

Forgetting her own problems for a moment, Karyn ventured, "You were like a sleeping princess, and then John woke you up?"

Fiona nodded. "And I'm staying awake. If I can defy my parents, you can flush that rotter Steve Patterson straight down the toilet."

Gentle, sweet-natured Fiona was scowling so fiercely that quite suddenly Karyn began to laugh. Fiona's scowl deepened. "Don't you laugh at me, Karyn Marshall—this has gone beyond a joke! Rafe's in pain, he's horribly unhappy. I can't stand seeing him so lost and all because you've locked yourself in the past and you're afraid of the future…I've got one more question, then I'll shut up."

Karyn knew what Fiona was going to ask. Did she, Karyn, love Rafe? How was she going to answer?

"Do you like Rafe, Karyn?"

"Like him?" Karyn said, surprised. "Yes…yes, of course I do."

"How can you like someone you're afraid of? You can't. It's impossible. I rest my case."

"You're wasted in the animal shelter," Karyn said vigorously. "You should be a high-powered lawyer—you could talk circles around any judge in the land."

"I like the animal shelter. I'm its new director and that's why I'm going home tomorrow, so I can be at work first thing on Monday morning."

Karyn bit her lip. "You left John behind on a weekend and came all this way to see me."

"To talk some sense into you."

Tears sparkling on her lashes, Karyn walked around the table and threw her arms around her sister. "Thank you, Fiona."

"Don't thank me," Fiona muttered, blinking back her own tears. "Go and see Rafe instead."

Karyn stepped back and straightened her spine. "Okay," she said, "I'll go and see him."

"You *will?*"

"I promise."

Fiona grabbed her twin and waltzed her around the tiny kitchen. "That's wonderful, that's terrific, I'm so glad."

"Rafe means an awful lot to you, doesn't he?"

Fiona raised expressive eyebrows. "Do horses have four legs?"

"Does he know you're here?"

"No, he took off to Thailand and won't be back until the end of next week. Late Friday night."

"Then I'll arrive on Saturday."

"I'll meet you at the Droverton station."

"Don't tell him, will you, Fiona?" Karyn said shakily. "I have to do this my way."

"I wouldn't think of telling him. Everyone in the village, including my parents, thinks I'm in London this weekend shopping for a wedding dress. Except for John, of course."

Karyn felt as though a whirlwind had picked her up, swirled her around and dropped her, disconcertingly, in a very different place. One where she wasn't sure she had her bearings. Fiona's wedding dress, she thought, surely that's a safe topic. "What sort of dress are you looking for?"

"I've got pictures."

The rest of the day, Fiona talked about John and about some of her youthful escapades with Rafe. Once the clinic had closed for the weekend, Karyn took her sister on a tour of the building, noticing how at ease Fiona was with all the animals. She ended the visit at the kennel of a mongrel called Toby; because Toby had been abused, he was reluctant to leave the safety of the kennel.

Kneeling beside Karyn, Fiona accepted a dog biscuit and

pushed it between the bars. "Come on, boy, you can do it," she coaxed, then smiled at Karyn. "Don't you think a nice tasty biscuit's worth the risk of leaving the cage?"

"Very funny."

"I don't mean to be funny—it takes a lot of guts to change things that went deep." She clucked at Toby as he sidled forward. The dog grabbed at the biscuit and retreated to chew on it. Then he came forward more confidently for another one. Within five minutes Toby was standing outside the kennel, with Fiona very gently massaging his shoulders. Karyn said softly, "He trusts you."

"Of course he does," Fiona said with a gamine grin. "Why wouldn't he?"

Why indeed? Fifteen minutes later, the mongrel was outdoors in the little field behind the clinic, sniffing at the grass and wagging his tail. Rafe would like to hear about Toby, Karyn thought.

She could tell him. On Saturday.

Had she really committed herself to visiting Droverton for the second time?

On Saturday afternoon Karyn landed at Heathrow. The plane was twenty minutes early; even so, she didn't have a lot of time to catch her train north. After going through customs in an agony of impatience, she hurried through the exit doors, tugging her wheeled suitcase.

An elderly couple stepped out of the crowd and approached her. The man was tall with a thatch of salt-and-pepper hair and bright blue eyes; his suit was unexceptional, although the trouser legs were tucked into blindingly red socks. The woman, short, rail-thin, was wearing an Indian cotton skirt and an old T-shirt; her eyes were almost black in a face that blended character and beauty to startling effect.

The man said bluffly, ''You're not Fiona, so you must be Karyn. Reginald Holden, m'dear, pleased to meet you.''

As he almost crushed her hand in his, the woman said, narrow-eyed, ''Are you here to see Rafe?''

''I'm on my way to Stoneriggs, yes—I'm in a hurry, I have to catch the train. Are you his mother?''

''He's not at Stoneriggs. He's here in London. Are you going to marry him?''

''Now, Joanie,'' said Reginald, ''that's not your question to ask.''

''Yes, it is, Reg. She's making our son miserable.''

''Irascible, I'd have said.''

''Same thing. Answer the question, girl.''

Karyn said coolly, ''My name's Karyn. I'm not a girl, I'm a woman. I don't know if I'm going to marry Rafe.''

Reginald gave a bark of laughter. ''She'll do,'' he said to his wife. ''That's what Rafe needs, someone to stand up to him.''

''He needs someone who loves him.''

''Can't expect him to be as lucky as you and me, m'dear.''

Reginald enveloped his wife in a bear hug; when she smiled up at him, Karyn's breath caught in her throat. She exclaimed, ''You're so lucky to love each other like that!''

''We're Rafe's parents, so we're scarcely objective,'' Joan announced. ''But we couldn't have a better son. If I'm not falling all over you, it's because you've hurt him deeply, and it makes me crazy not to be able to fix it.''

''My husband wasn't a nice man,'' Karyn said with careful understatement.

''We're all entitled to the occasional mistake,'' Reginald said breezily. ''Jolly good thing the chap's out of the way.''

Karyn raised her brows. ''That's one way of looking at it.''

Joan said fiercely, ''You're breaking Rafe's heart. You've got to choose one thing or the other—waste your life in fear and regret, or get on with it.''

''Wallow in the mud,'' Reginald said cheerfully, ''or climb back on the horse that threw you.''

''I packed my jodphurs,'' Karyn said.

''Then you're all set,'' Reginald replied. ''After all, she's here, isn't she, Joanie? That's got to count for something. She doesn't live in the next county, you know.''

''Do you love my son?'' Joan asked in a voice like a steel blade. A voice that reminded Karyn strongly of Rafe.

''I don't know,'' she replied, refusing to drop her eyes. ''But I'm willing to try and find out. Providing you'll tell where in London I can find him.''

Joan passed her a crumpled invitation. ''He's got a gala opening of a new hotel tonight—here's the address. You could attend. If you wanted to.''

''I'll do that,'' Karyn said. ''You could wish me luck. If you wanted to.''

Joan nodded, as though Karyn's answers had pleased her. ''Something dies inside us when we don't take risks,'' she remarked. ''You probably know that, or you wouldn't be here.''

''Are you going to the gala?'' Karyn asked.

''We've got a sick dog at home, so we have to get back—we commandeered Rafe's helicopter so we could meet you.''

Karyn said, smiling for the first time, ''I'm honored you left the dog just to see me.''

Then a blur of movement caught her eye; Fiona, wearing a pretty blue suit, was pushing through the crowd toward her. Karyn said in happy surprise, ''Fiona, how lovely to see you.''

Fiona stopped dead, gaping at Rafe's parents. ''What are

you doing here?'' she said tactlessly. Her eyes widened. ''You were asking about Karyn last night—picking my brains. I just hope you haven't been giving her a hard time.''

''Came to check her out,'' Reginald said.

''She's not a prize filly,'' Fiona said crossly and gave Karyn a distracted kiss on the cheek. ''So you know Rafe's in London? I only found out this morning. I was so afraid I'd miss you and you'd be on your way to Droverton... although I wouldn't have worried if I'd known Reg and Joan were planning to be here,'' she finished, frowning at them.

''We knew you wouldn't want us interfering,'' Joan said briskly. ''So we didn't tell you.''

''This is getting much too complicated,'' Fiona complained. ''Karyn, I didn't bring John with me because I thought you'd be in a tizzy. You can meet him when you come home with Rafe after the gala.''

''It's not a tizzy, it's a funk,'' Karyn said, ''and you're making one heck of a big assumption about Rafe and me.'' She hugged her sister fiercely. ''No matter what happens, I'm so glad to see you, and thanks so much for coming all this way—it's getting to be a habit, rescuing me like this.''

''I won't have to do it any more, because once you see Rafe you won't need rescuing,'' Fiona said triumphantly.

''How is he, Fiona?'' Karyn burst out.

''I talked to him this morning at the hotel—he didn't sound in a very gala mood. But he'll feel a million percent better when he sees you,'' Fiona said. ''How's Toby?''

''He has new owners—a wonderful couple who live in the country and love him to bits. He's a different dog.''

''He's a walking metaphor, that dog,'' Fiona said with a sideways grin.

Karyn hoped so. But even if she herself had changed

enough to come in search of Rafe, what if he didn't want to see her? What if he was so angry with her that he turned his back on her? Wouldn't that serve her right?

Worse, what if he'd changed his mind? It was fine for Fiona and Joan to insist Rafe was still in love with her. But what did they know? Maybe all those feelings he'd talked about had been brought on by too much Greek sunshine and an overdose of sex.

Then there were her own feelings. Was she in love with him? Or would she have to rebuild trust before she'd know?

All her doubts and fears must have shown in her face. "Karyn, it'll be fine. With Rafe, I mean," Fiona said forcefully.

"Maybe," said Karyn, "and maybe not. But I have to see him, no matter what. I couldn't live with myself if I didn't." She hesitated. "Fiona, I don't want to send you away. But I've got to do this on my own…do you understand?"

"Of course I do! You don't need the whole darn family tagging along…by the way, I booked a room for you at Rafe's hotel. It's next door to some incredible boutiques, in case you didn't bring anything to wear."

Tears on her lashes, Karyn said, "You've thought of everything."

"The rest is up to you," Fiona said. "You can do it."

Reginald interjected, "Fiona, you could come back with us in the 'copter. You'll be home in no time." He gave Karyn a courtly bow. "Best of luck, m'dear. Drop by the castle for tea, why don't you?"

Joan kissed Karyn on the cheek, a gesture that felt like an accolade. "That way you can meet the dogs."

"I'd like that," Karyn said.

She hugged Fiona again, then watched as the three of them disappeared through the jostle of other passengers.

Her first step was to get a taxi to the hotel, where she was going to gate-crash a very fancy gala.

Hosted by Rafe.

CHAPTER ELEVEN

AS THE cab wound through the London streets in a series of jerky stops and starts, Karyn could hear, far in the distance and overriding the sound of traffic, the grumble of thunder. The sky between the tall buildings was heaped with purple-edged clouds; the trees were whipped by a wind that whirled dust from the gutters and tossed scraps of paper into the air. If she were back home, she'd say they were in for a storm. She was trying very hard not to see this as a bad omen.

She was wearing her expensive linen slacks with a blue linen blazer and an ivory silk blouse; as the taxi lurched forward, she did her best to repair her makeup. In her case, carefully packed in tissue, was the delphinium-blue dress Rafe had given her in Greece. She'd brought it hoping that he'd strip it from her body and make love to her, just as he had once before in their big bedroom that overlooked Cape Sounio. But instead she'd be wearing it to the most momentous confrontation of her life.

The crumpled piece of paper Joan had given her said the gala began with cocktails at seven. Karyn was already praying she wouldn't bump into Rafe before it began; she wanted him to see her first in the midst of the invited guests. That way he'd have more time to cool down. Less time to consider homicide, she thought wryly. He couldn't very well send her packing in front of everyone. Could he?

He could try. It didn't mean she had to obey him.

Lightning flickered between two office towers. The cabbie slipped through an opening in the traffic, the mete clicking with monotonous regularity. Her eyes scratchy from lack of sleep, because she'd been up since four that morning, Karyn gazed out at crowded pavements and red double-decker buses, at stone and brick architecture rooted in history. She might be scared to death of meeting Rafe; but she was also unable to quell a tremor of excitement that she was finally in London, a city that for her had always been wreathed in romance.

Briefly her overstretched nerves loosened. Perhaps she'd come home, she thought. Maybe England was where she belonged, with a man as civilized as this great city, as unyielding as the granite crags of his estate, as wild and powerful as the windtorn sky. Were he to love her, were she to allow that love to permeate her, and were she to return it, strength for strength…was that why she was here? To find out what that would be like?

With one final jolt, the cab drew up in front of an elegant Edwardian stone building, lights gleaming from its myriad windows. Quickly Karyn paid the fare, added a generous tip and got out. Trundling her bag behind her, she walked toward the huge arched entranceway, where a uniformed doorman greeted her as though she was royalty, took her bag and indicated the front desk.

For a moment, awestruck, her steps faltered. She was standing under a domed ceiling centred with a magnificent gold chandelier; the ivory walls were outlined in gilt, the ceiling a baroque marvel of swirled gold and exquisite murals. A bouquet of tropical lilies rested on a marble pedestal; the floors were pale marble, the carpets handloomed. With all the dignity at her command, she approached the desk and within moments was being whisked in the elevator to her room on the fifth floor.

She hadn't seen Rafe.

She had two hours to get ready.

Staying even one night in this room was going to wreck her budget for the next twelve months; all the more reason to enjoy it while she was here. Recklessly Karyn ordered afternoon tea to be brought to her room, even though according to her it was only lunchtime. When it came on a mahogany trolley with immaculate linens, she tucked into tiny sandwiches and luscious little cakes, pouring Prince of Wales tea from an antique silver pot.

Perched on her bed, she looked around her. Silk-damask upholstery and drapes, a deeply piled carpet in forest-green, dark cherry furnishings, two delicate prints of dancers: every detail was perfect. She'd already checked out the marble bathroom with its fleecy robe and lavish toiletries.

Having consumed every scrap of food, she soaked in fragrant bubbles in the whirlpool tub, painted her nails, and took her time making up her face. When she was finally ready, at quarter past seven, she took one last look at herself in the mirror.

A glamorous stranger looked back at her, a woman with delicately flushed cheeks and brilliant blue eyes, her hair in soft tendrils around her face. Crystal earrings twinkled at her lobes; the blue dress encased her like the petals of a slender flower.

The only thing missing was the gold chain with the teardrop diamond that she'd sent back to Rafe.

She tilted her chin. She was going downstairs, she was going to find Rafe, and she was going to fight for him. In fighting for him, she'd be fighting for her own life. Defeating Steve, once and for all.

Freeing herself to be with Rafe. If he'd have her.

She tucked her door card in her silver clutch purse, and left the room. Five minutes later, she was standing at the entrance to the lobby bar. A group of guests was ahead of her, giving her a moment to get her bearings.

Small gold lamps cast a warm glow on the deep red walls, giving the polished walnut trim a lovely sheen. Intricately woven carpets were scattered on an expanse of gleaming parquet. The room was already crowded with men in tuxedos, the women's gowns a mingling of hues like a midsummer garden. White-jacketed waiters moved smoothly among the guests.

Rafe was standing with his back to her, talking to several men and one woman, a brunette whose beauty and sophistication Karyn couldn't hope to emulate. Even from here she could see diamonds in a sparkling cascade around the woman's throat. For a moment Karyn quailed. What if Rafe had indeed put her behind him? A regrettable interlude, the sooner forgotten the better.

What if this woman was his new partner? Or even his partner for the evening?

She'd been a fool to come.

*You're breaking his heart…*so Joan had said and so Fiona had suggested. As he laughed, bending his head to hear what the woman was saying, he didn't look as though his heart was broken.

"Your name, madam?"

The doorman, in a scarlet jacket and a high starched collar, was addressing her. "Dr. Karyn Marshall," Karyn said clearly. She rarely used her title; but this seemed an occasion that called for it.

He ran his eyes down the list in his hand. "I don't believe your name is here," he said delicately. "Could there have been some mistake?"

Gate-crashers. Jewel thieves. Unwanted interlopers. Of course there'd be security for an event of this size. "I flew in at the last minute from Canada," she said. "If you mention my name to Mr. Holden, I'm sure he'll be delighted to welcome me."

"Certainly, madam."

The doorman made an unobtrusive gesture to one of the waiters and whispered instructions in his ear. The waiter walked across the parquet toward Rafe, discreetly got his attention and spoke to him very briefly. For a split second Rafe's body went utterly still. Then he said something to the waiter and turned back to his guests.

Not once did he look Karyn's way.

All right, Rafe, she thought in a wave of fury. If that's your game, I can play it, too.

The waiter returned and the doorman said with impeccable courtesy, gesturing her into the room, "Enjoy your evening, madam."

She planned to. Her blood up, Karyn helped herself to a chilled martini from one of the waiters and took the first sip, its bite almost making her choke. A man standing nearby said, with amusement, "They're extremely good martinis."

He was handsome and gray-haired, with that indescribable polish that generations of wealth can confer. Karyn introduced herself, and soon discovered he was laird of a vast estate in Scotland and had a keen interest in sheep-breeding. As they talked animatedly, he said, "Let me introduce you to those three gentlemen over there…they'd like to hear your views on Cheviots."

The three men were standing close to Rafe. Sipping her martini with caution, for she needed all her wits about her, Karyn crossed the room and joined the three men. Even then Rafe paid her no attention whatsoever. We'll see about that, she thought, waited for a gap in the conversation and said pleasantly to her companions, "Would you excuse me, please? I want to speak to Mr. Holden."

Holding herself very tall, she closed the gap until she

stood at Rafe's elbow, then said clearly, ''Good evening, Rafe.''

He turned, his glance flicking over her face. ''Dr. Marshall,'' he said. ''What an unexpected pleasure.''

''They're the best kind, don't you think?'' she said, and smiled at the other guests. She was damned if she was going to show that his use of her last name had flicked her like a lash.

Rafe said imperturbably, ''May I introduce Dr. Karyn Marshall.'' He reeled off the others' names, not one of which Karyn could have repeated, although she did catch that the brunette was the wife of the handsome aristocrat standing across from Rafe.

Calling on every ounce of her poise, she talked and laughed and smiled until she thought her jaw would crack. Then Rafe said, ''Ah, the ambassador's party has arrived…please excuse me. Karyn, I'll see you later.''

Briefly his eyes rested on her with a such a blaze of emotion that she almost dropped her glass. So he wasn't indifferent to her. Far from it. She said coolly, ''Perhaps.''

''It's not a suggestion, it's an order.'' His smile impar-ially included the whole group. ''Karyn and I have some unfinished business,'' he remarked, took her hand, kissed her palm with lingering pleasure and walked away from her.

Scorched by the contact, her cheeks flaming, Karyn said, 'He's exaggerating and he's much too used to having his own way. I need another martini.''

The brunette, whose name was Lydia, signaled the waiter. ''Rafe is never indiscreet,'' she said, ''how inter-sting. Where did you meet him, Karyn?''

Karyn had no intention of sharing a convoluted story about separated twins and a picnic on a faraway beach. ''By chance,'' she said, and to her great relief heard the doorman announce that dinner was ready to be served.

Now was her opportunity to leave with some degree of dignity. But hadn't Steve destroyed every vestige of her fighting spirit? Was she going to run away from Rafe and that blaze of emotion he'd banked as swiftly as if it had never occurred; or was she going to match him, thrust for thrust, parry for parry? His opponent and his equal.

Steadily she walked with Lydia and her husband toward the dining room. Its gold-framed mirrors reflected the dazzle of chandeliers and gold-leaf tracery on walls of a soft moss green. An array of crystal glasses shot little rainbows on the circular tables with their bouquets of roses and tall gold candelabra. At the door, the maitre d' took her name and said politely, ''Ah yes, Dr. Marshall…you're on Mr Holden's right at the head table.''

She said with the utmost composure, ''Thank you,'' winked at Lydia and crossed the room toward the long table flanked by twin marble fireplaces. Her heart was fluttering in her breast; so this was Rafe's next move. He'd outguessed her; she'd expected to be seated in a corner as far from him as possible.

On her other side was a charming French count whose passion, she soon found out, was horse racing. From the corner of her eye she saw Rafe approach. ''Mr. Holden,'' she said with edgy mockery, ''what an unexpected pleasure.''

''I thought I could keep an eye on you here,'' he said.

''Do you like my dress?'' she asked provocatively.

''A pity you don't have a gold chain to go with it.''

''Flinging down the gauntlet—what a romantic gesture that is.''

''I'm not sure what I'm feeling right now, but romantic doesn't cut it.''

She widened her eyes, aware that she was thoroughly enjoying herself. ''So I shouldn't pin my hopes on having had my hand kissed?''

His gaze lingered on the soft curve of her mouth. ''It depends what your hopes are. We'll discuss them later—when we're alone.'' Turning to the woman on his left, he said, ''Countess, may I introduce Dr. Karyn Marshall?''

Valiantly Karyn held up her end of the conversation, working her way through Beluga caviar, delicately flavored bouillon, flame-roasted quail, and pastries shaped like swans surrounded by plump raspberries. Rafe made a speech notable for wit and brevity, then everyone moved to the baroque splendor of the ballroom, where the orchestra was tuning their instruments.

Karyn, by now, was light-headed with fatigue, wine, repressed sexuality and suspense. Rafe led off the dancing, taking her into his arms and sweeping her around the floor in an old-fashioned waltz. His arm around her waist, his fingers clasping her own to his shoulder, the closeness of his determined jaw and unfathomable dark eyes all worked their magic. Her body yielded in his arms in a way that spoke volumes. He said harshly, ''So that hasn't changed.''

''Did you expect it to?''

''I've given up knowing what to expect from you.''

His fingers were now splayed over her hip in overt possessiveness. How important was Steve likened to the elemental simplicity of Rafe's embrace? It was Rafe who matched her, body and soul. Rafe who from the beginning had shown her that passion could be coupled with integrity, willpower with trust.

What a fool she'd been to compare him to Steve. In all the ways that mattered, there was no comparison. How could she have forgotten the first time Rafe had made love to her, in the bungalow in Maine? He'd put his own needs on hold in order to soothe her fears and bring her to fulfillment. He'd been breathtakingly generous.

Yet she'd run from him like a terrified sheep.

Not paying attention, she stepped on his toe. "Sorry," she muttered.

"Only another three hours," he said heartlessly. "I have to circulate…I'll pass you over to the count."

Soon Karyn was whirling around the dance floor with a succession of partners young and old. Normally she would have enjoyed this immensely. But as the minutes and hours passed, the knot in her belly tightened. Rafe hadn't danced with her again. Nor did she have any idea what she was going to say to him when, as he'd promised, they found themselves alone.

Promised or threatened, she wondered with a shiver along her spine.

For the second time she watched him lead a frail, white-haired dowager onto the floor, dancing with her with such care for her pleasure that sudden tears shimmered on Karyn's lashes. As she rubbed them away, it was as though she rubbed scales from her eyes.

She loved Rafe. Of course she did.

She had for weeks.

Her new knowledge didn't arrive in a blinding flash, like the lightning flickering over the city streets. It held none of the threat of a stormy sky. Rather, it had the integrity of Rafe's beloved Stoneriggs, and the deep roots of her connection to Fiona. It was as dependable as stone, she thought; as beautiful as the sea. She could feel her heart expanding to encompass him, to hold him there forever. Happiness welled up within her.

She loved him. Now she must tell him so.

The orchestra announced the last waltz. With a sense of inevitability, Karyn watched Rafe return the dowager to her equally aged husband and then swiftly search the crowd. For herself. Talking and laughing as he went, he eased his way toward her and took her in his arms.

I love Rafe, she thought. That's all I need to remember. The rest will look after itself.

I hope.

But she couldn't recapture the delight of being in his arms. Twice she tripped over her own feet; her body felt clumsy, her brain empty of any kind of strategy. Finally the waltz ended; as the guests started to depart and Rafe began a round of goodbyes, she slipped into the ladies room and repaired her makeup. Lipstick for courage, she thought ruefully, running a comb through her tangled curls. She didn't look like a woman who'd been up for twenty-one hours. She looked fully and invigoratingly alive.

When she went back out, the great ballroom was nearly empty, the musicians putting away their instruments as the staff cleared the tables of used glasses. The party's over, she thought, and slowly walked over to Rafe, who was shaking hands with the last of the guests.

As though he sensed her presence, he turned. His face inscrutable, he said, ''Let's go.''

Deliberately she laced her arm with his, feeling the muscles rigid as steel beneath the sleeve of his tuxedo. They crossed the lobby to the elevators. The attendant pressed the button for the penthouse suite, and in silence they were whooshed upward. Rafe unlocked tall double doors and stood aside for her to enter.

In one quick glance, she took in her surroundings. Space and simplicity, she thought with a sigh of relief. ''Is this your own suite?''

''Yes. We won't be disturbed here. Why did you come to London?''

So there was to be no social chitchat. Karyn sat down

on the arm of the nearest chair and eased her stiletto sandals off her feet. "I came to see you."

"Why?"

I've all of a sudden realized I love you? It didn't sound very convincing. "You don't look too happy that I'm here."

"The jury's out on that one. How did you know where to find me?"

"Your mother told me." With a flick of satisfaction she saw she had surprised him. "If I can get past your mother, you should be congratulating me."

"Just how did you meet her?"

"She was at the airport, waiting for me. She gave me the third degree. I like your father's socks."

"Stick to the point, Karyn."

"You're not making this very easy!"

"Give me one good reason why I should. I've just had the worst two weeks of my whole life. When Celine fouled me up, that was kidstuff compared to you. So I don't feel particularly friendly toward you, and if you try to compare me to Steve one more time, we're through—have you got that?"

Her visions of a romantic late-night tryst in ruins at her feet, Karyn let her own temper rise to meet his. "You're not the least bit like Steve."

"Then why did you send me away?" he snarled.

"Isn't it obvious? Because I hadn't figured that out yet."

"So you sent me packing along with the necklace I'd given you—you wouldn't even keep that."

"I'm sorry!" she cried, then modulated her tone. "I really am sorry, Rafe. I did the best I could at the time—and it wasn't good enough. I see that now. But hindsight's always twenty-twenty and I came here to make amends. Well, that's sort of why I came."

''I laid my cards on the table at Heathrow,'' Rafe said in a harsh voice. ''I love you, I want to marry you—that's what I said. Causing you to bolt like a frightened pony. Good move, Rafe. I might be a dab hand at building a business empire but when it comes to one five-foot-seven blue-eyed blonde, I'm—''

''Oh, stop!'' she yelped. ''You know what I really want to ask? Do you still love me? Do you still want to marry me? But I'm not going to. I'm going to say my piece first. I love you, Rafe Holden. I want to marry you. That's why I'm here, and if I could get past your redoubtable mother, you ought to be down on your knees kissing my feet.''

''I'm damned if I'm getting down on my knees—I did that at Heathrow. What changed your mind? Why all of a sudden aren't I the reincarnation of Steve?''

''It's a long story.''

''I've got all night.''

Panic-stricken, because her declaration of love might as well have been spoken to the four corners of the room, Karyn began by describing how Fiona had turned up on her doorstep last Saturday morning in a rage. ''You should have seen her—maybe she's been taking lessons from your mother. Anyway, I promised I'd come here as soon as I could, and…well, see you. I guess that's what I promised.''

''You're seeing me. Right now.''

''Did I ruin everything by sending you away?'' Karyn croaked. ''Oh, please, tell me I didn't…''

''You answer me first. Am I dreaming this whole scene? This whole evening? Any minute am I going to wake up in a bed that feels like a desert because you're not in it?''

''I'm real.'' She reached out and touched him, snatching her hand back before he could react.

''So you are. You love me,'' he said, advancing one step

toward her, "and you want to marry me. You did say that?"

His eyes were gleaming with something other than anger; the first tiny quiver of hope rippled through her body. "Yes," she said primly, "and it's not even a leap year."

"I accept."

"Huh?"

"I accept your proposal of marriage," he repeated, "and I'll make damn sure our grandchildren know it was you who asked me and not the other way around."

"You asked first."

"Don't remind me. When are we going to get married? It had better be soon."

"Whoa," she said, "you're leaving something out. Something basic. If you don't love me any more, the proposal's off."

"Oh, I love you," Rafe said softly, taking one more step. He was now so close she could feel the heat of his body and see the tiny flames deep in his eyes. "Do you think I'd change that quickly? That's the whole point, Karyn. I'm in this for life. Forever. For better and for worse, and since Heathrow I've had more than enough of the worse, thank you very much."

A smile lighting her eyes, she said severely, "You're playing very hard to get."

"You're darn right I am. Although if you got past my mother, maybe, just maybe, I should forgive you."

She laughed, a delightful cascade of sound. "You're darn right you should."

Still without touching her, his voice deepening, Rafe said, "I love you, Karyn. Love you more deeply than I knew it was possible to love. I want you to be my wife, to be the mother of our children, to live with me day by day, to sleep in my bed." The little flames kindled to points of fire. "To make love with me again and again, because I'll never have enough of you.''

Her face radiant, Karyn whispered, ''That's what I want, too. More than I can say.'' Then, very naturally, she moved into the circle of his arms, linked her hands behind his head and kissed him.

It was a kiss that seemed to last forever, an avowal of love, an ache of desire, a pledge of belonging. When Karyn finally raised her head, her cheeks were bright pink. She said the first thing that came into her mind. ''Rafe, I'm so sorry I sent you away.''

''You're forgiven,'' he said and kissed her again.

Through the windows that opened onto the balcony, Karyn heard the faraway growl of thunder. ''We're in for a storm.''

Rafe laughed, his white teeth gleaming. ''We are the storm, sweetheart.'' When he ran his eyes down her body, it felt as intimate as a caress. ''Let's go to bed.''

''Yes,'' she whispered, ''oh, yes.''

''When you look at me like that—'' He pulled her hard into his body, smothering her face and throat with hot, urgent kisses. ''I want you, I need you, I love you.''

Karyn rested her palm on Rafe's cheek, smiling into his eyes. ''I love you, too,'' she said. ''Oh, Rafe, I love you so much.''

''That's all you have to do—keep telling me that for the rest of my days.''

''That's easy,'' Karyn said contentedly, reaching up to unhook his tie. He swung her off her feet, carrying her through the sitting room into the bedroom with its panorama of city lights. Laying her on her back, he covered her with his big body.

She was home. In Rafe's bed, in his heart. Where she belonged.

* * *

A month later, on a Friday evening, Karyn was maid of honor and Rafe best man at Fiona and John's wedding in the thick-walled Norman church in Droverton. On Saturday afternoon, Karyn was standing at the end of the same aisle, her hand tucked into John's sleeve as the organ pealed the wedding march. Her gown was an elegant flow of white crepe, her bouquet exquisite lilies from Joan's conservatory at Castle Holden. The diamond pendant Rafe had given her in Greece hung on its delicate gold chain around her neck.

Fiona, wearing apple-green crepe, turned to smile at her. "Your turn," she said. "May you be as happy as I am, Karyn."

"It's because of you that I'm standing here."

"It's because of Rafe."

Karyn could see him at the far end of the aisle, his black hair uncharacteristically tidy, his morning suit molded to his broad shoulders. Joy spilled over in her heart. She leaned forward and kissed her sister on the cheek. Then she smiled at John, whom she already liked enormously. "Ready?" she asked.

"Be happy, Karyn," he said.

"I will be. I am."

She paced slowly up the aisle, the stained glass throwing a mosaic of brilliant colors on the guests. Clarissa and Douglas, valiantly smiling; Rafe's mother, severely elegant in bottle-green silk; Reginald enlivening his formal clothes with an orange bowtie.

Her new family.

Also among the guests were Liz, Pierre and their children, whom Rafe had brought here to surprise her: a gift that had, predictably, made her weep.

Then Rafe himself turned to find her, his dark blue eyes meeting hers with such an immensity of tenderness that her heart overflowed. She took her place at his side. In a few moments Rafe would be her husband and she his wife.

She'd freed herself from the past. Freed herself to a life-long commitment with Rafe and, she hoped, to bearing his children. She could ask for nothing more.

Resting her hand on Rafe's, she smiled up at him, and as the music swelled around her, the future began.